Devil's Breath Volcano

Devil's Breath Volcano

MacGregor Family
Adventure Series
Book Six

a novel by

Richard Trout

PELICAN PUBLISHING COMPANY
GRETNA 2008

The word "Pelican" and the depiction of a pelican
are trademarks of Pelican Publishing Company, Inc.,
and are registered in the U.S. Patent and Trademark Office.

ISBN-13: 978-1-58980-558-3
Library of Congress Control Number: 2008007314

The entirety of this novel is a work of fiction and bears no resemblance to real people or events. The MacGregor teens perform daring deeds that should not be attempted by any minor without the advice and consent of an adult.

Printed in the United States of America

Published by Pelican Publishing Company, Inc.
1000 Burmaster Street, Gretna, Louisiana 70053

For
Steve, Margo, Evan, Angie,
&
Ethan Funk

Great Kansans All!

Contents

Acknowledgments

Special thanks to Dr. Neal Coates (political scientist); my first dive instructor in 1970, the late Frank Best Thompson; Virginia May, who let me hang out in Huntington Beach so I could learn how to dive California style; and the talented artist for all of my covers, Aundrea Hernandez.

Devil's Breath Volcano

Prologue

South Pacific, March 1944

―――――――――――――〇――――――――――――――

The two silver P-38 fighters had been on a reconnaissance mission for much longer than they had planned. As members of the 339th Fighter Squadron of the 347th Fighter Group, Thirteenth Air Force, they were deep in Japanese occupied territory in the South Pacific just north of the giant Japanese naval base at Rabaul. The flight from the U.S. air base on New Guinea to the site of the Japanese fleet was much farther than the U.S. Navy PBY Catalina had earlier reported. Even with two big Allison engines with a seven hundred-mile range, the P-38s had been extending their time over the Bismarck Sea, passing over New Ireland, a Japanese stronghold. Running low on fuel, they began to scan the seas for a flat atoll that was big enough to land where they could wait for refueling. Suddenly the skies erupted in puffs of black smoke with large bangs that rocked their aircraft.

Peering down through the clouds around them, they realized they had flown over a small fleet of Japanese cruisers, tankers, and troop ships steaming to the naval base at

Rabaul to reinforce the weary Imperial Japanese Army. The
antiaircraft guns on the ships began to hammer the clouds,
hoping that a piece of shrapnel would luckily pierce a fuel
tank and down the two American fighters.

"Shark's Leader Two, did you see that?"

"Roger, Outlaw. Guess we can't land down there right
now," Shark's Leader Two replied.

"Roger, wait, I think I just got hit. I'm losing some oil out
of the starboard engine. Yep, there goes the red light.
Losing altitude," Outlaw said as he rolled the P-38 over on
its side to drop out of the clouds and into full view of the
Japanese ships below.

As he rolled, he looked to his right and saw an emerald
green coral island to the south of the Japanese ships. Later
he would learn that it was Simbari Island.

"I'm pointing her toward that island down there. Run
some interference for me," Outlaw said.

"Roger, Outlaw. Maybe they'll retrain their guns my way,"
Shark's Leader Two said and banked the opposite direction.

Shark's Leader Two's P-38 did catch the attention of the
small battle group, and they redirected their fire as Outlaw
went into a dive. Lt. Gary Bridwell, U.S. Army Air Corps,
could not believe his eyes when he leveled out at the same
moment a Japanese heavy cruiser was clearing the end of
the atoll. Bridwell flew his wounded plane right at it.
Without hesitation, he dropped down to the deck, the surface of the ocean, and took aim at the ten thousand-ton
cruiser *Kako Maru.* Just barely skimming the ocean waves,
he came in head-on to the Japanese ship too low for her
deck guns to sight in on him. As he engaged the trigger on
his 20mm canon, he pulled up just enough to strafe the
tower and shatter all of the windows in front of the
Japanese naval command. Five of the officers were hit and
dropped dead instantly with the others diving for cover. As
he flew the P-38 straight down the main deck, he noticed a
Japanese submarine moored to the portside of the ship

trailing oil. Suddenly the main deck exploded. The fireball jumped into the sky as the ship began to blow apart.

"Shark's Leader Two, this is Outlaw. Looks like I got another one, and she's going down."

"Good shooting. But before you break your arm patting your back, you should know I spotted a torpedo in the water on the starboard side just before the explosion. Must be a friendly sub down there," Shark's Leader Two said.

"Thanks for the confidence. I think I found a landing strip on the beach. It looks like it's a mile long and winds may be just right. Peel off from the fight and head home. We don't need two pilots stranded out here," Outlaw responded.

"Roger, but I can't figure out this Japanese submarine action. They're frantically trying to separate, but it looks like it's too late. She's going down with the cruiser. Their unlucky day, I suppose," Shark's Leader Two replied as he began to circle well out of range of the ships.

"Outlaw, looks like they're continuing southward. You'll be safe so just lay low. I'm going to radio in coordinates as soon as I'm far enough away so the Japs don't decide to send in a force after you," he said.

"Good thinking, Shark's Leader. I'm sure they would come after me if they thought about it long enough. O.K., I'm touching down, good traction, beach slope is minimal, see you later Bill. Outlaw out," Bridwell responded, fighting to keep the aircraft straight on the wide beach of the island with his starboard engine shutting off just after touch down.

"You picked one with a sizeable peak, probably an old volcano. That will help with the rescue. See you soon," Capt. William Pfleiderer said and pointed his P-38 toward the secure allied landing strip on the Solomon Islands to the southeast.

The silver P-38, nicknamed by the Nazis as the forked-tail devil, whizzed down the beach with the pilot pulling hard on the rudder to correct for the slant of the ground, one dead engine, and a crosswind. The idea was to keep the plane dry.

As Bridwell reached the end of the beach next to the lagoon, he saw a break in the palm trees and drove the P-38 between them into a small clearing in a grove of trees and tropical plants. As the prop spun to a stop, he crawled out of the cockpit and stepped out onto the wing. He unfastened his parachute and tossed it into the open canopy. He quickly drew out his army-issue Colt .45 and loaded a round in the chamber, listening for any sound. Confident there were no enemy troops close by, he holstered the pistol and jumped to the ground.

Once on the ground, he walked down to the beach where he could see the wounded cruiser break through the barrier reef into the lagoon about a thousand yards from the beach. The small submarine slipped beneath the waves first, with the larger cruiser crushing down on top of it as it flipped over on its side. Bridwell thought for a minute that he might have company, but a series of explosions soon took care of that, or so he hoped. He sat down on the beach and watched until the last vestige of the Japanese warship was submerged two hours later. Lucky for him the lagoon's deepest end was exactly where the ship had crushed through the coral reef and entered the lagoon, or the cruiser would still be sitting half out of the water.

He walked back to the P-38 and climbed up to the cockpit where he reached inside and retrieved a small shoulder bag that contained basic first-aid supplies, C rations, and replacement ammunition for the Colt .45 he had holstered under his left shoulder. He found one quart-size tin full of fresh water and knew right away that finding more water would be his biggest challenge.

Suddenly he heard the roar of another P-38 overhead. Bridwell looked up and immediately recognized the numbers of Shark's Leader Two and that his fuselage was on fire and smoking heavily.

The wounded fighter made a sharp bank at the end of the lagoon and then dropped to within three feet of the water.

Capt. William Pfleiderer lowered his landing gear, and the P-38 hit the water and was quickly pulled in nose first, creating a huge column of water that rushed across the top of the cockpit dousing the fire.

Bridwell's heart pounded rapidly as he watched the warplane begin to sink to the bottom of the lagoon. He started running down the beach to a spot parallel to where the plane went down. When he got there, he was reaching down to pull off his flight boots when Shark's Leader Two's head popped up in the blue lagoon. Bridwell yelled and waved, and Pfleiderer waved back and began to swim to the beach.

Within a few minutes, he was walking out of the tropical surf. The men embraced as they met.

"Great landing," Lieutenant Bridwell said.

"Thanks. That one they don't teach in army flight school. Only the navy boys get that kind of training," Captain Pfleiderer replied and began to pull off his wet gear.

"How'd you get hit?" Bridwell asked as they began walking back toward the P-38 in the clearing.

"I made it about an hour from here, and then my engine started smoking. I must have taken a hit when you did, but it was a slow leak. I didn't know how far I could make it so my best chance was to turn around and come back. I followed the smoke trail left by the sinking cruiser. Thank goodness she was slow going down. Are there any survivors we're going to have to deal with?" Pfleiderer asked.

"I didn't see any swim away or make it to shore," Bridwell replied. "But there was a lot of smoke."

"Good. Does your radio still work?" Pfleiderer asked.

"Yes it does, but we'll need to wait a few hours to let the Japanese ships get farther away. We don't need any angry Japanese coming back to get even," Bridwell said.

"I agree. Let's get the P-38 camouflaged so it's not spotted by a Japanese patrol plane. This island is sitting right on the main naval corridor of the Bismarck Archipelago and New Guinea," Pfleiderer said as they reached the fighter plane.

"Our lucky day," Bridwell replied.

The two aviators began ripping and tearing foliage and tossing it over the wings first. Then they built up piles of palm leaves until they had covered the fuselage and tail sections. As the sun set in the west, they bedded down on the big fronds of palms covering the beach and shared the container of fresh water.

Three hours of darkness had passed when a splashing noise down the beach awakened them both. The pilots were trained soldiers so they moved carefully and quietly to look up from where they had been sleeping. The moon was full, and the beach was illumined for a hundred yards.

"Japanese sailors in a raft," Bridwell whispered and reached for his Colt .45.

"I count five or six," Pfleiderer said and pulled his gun out from under the palm fronds.

"I bet they escaped from the submarine. Looks like they're going to camp on the beach tonight, which means by daylight we'll be in full view," Bridwell whispered.

"That's for sure. Let's move slowly into the tree line. Inch in there carefully. Keep your gun ready," Pfleiderer said, being the senior officer by one grade.

Carefully and at a snail's pace the aviators pulled and pushed their bodies across the soft sand that seemed more like powdered sugar. After an hour of crawling, they had only moved fifty feet and were now behind a continuous row of palms. The six men of the Imperial Japanese Navy had started a fire and were busily eating and drinking from the supplies they had brought with them.

"They're going to find the aircraft first thing in the morning, and there goes our radio," Lieutenant Bridwell said sullenly.

"Not if we go down there and neutralize them," Captain Pfleiderer replied.

The two pilots took their Colt .45 automatics in their left hands and grasped their right arms together.

"Good luck," Pfleiderer said.

"Same here," Bridwell replied.

"Check your weapon, and be sure the exchange is clear of any sand. We've got three full clips each," Pfleiderer said.

"That's enough for our own little war," his wingman replied.

"We've got two approach choices. Move down the tree line quietly or back out to the lagoon and come in from the water side," Pfleiderer noted.

"I vote for the tree line," Bridwell answered.

"I agree. The moon is too bright for a sea assault. Let's go," Pfleiderer said.

The two aviators moved deeper into the tropical foliage taking each step carefully. On the occasion they stepped on a dry branch and heard a snap, they would freeze to see if the Japanese had heard the noise. Checking their watches, they had moved through the tree line in roughly an hour and were now about fifty feet from the campfire and the sleeping Japanese.

Pfleiderer held up his left hand and motioned that there were six men, all with weapons. Bridwell nodded, and they moved within thirty feet of the enemy. Neither pilot had made a noise, but one of the Japanese sat up quickly and looked around. He unholstered his Nambu Type 14 8mm pistol, loaded a cartridge, and released the safety. The Americans pointed their Colts directly at the sailor who they could now see was wearing an officer's uniform.

The Japanese officer poked at two others quickly, and they awoke in a stir. He put his index finger to his lips, signaling for them to be quiet. Pfleiderer pointed to Bridwell and motioned for him to take the one on the right and he would take the one on the left. Bridwell nodded and came up partway out of his crouch. A dry branch snapped under his flight boots, and the Japanese started yelling orders at the sleeping men. Within seconds, all six men were awake and brandishing their weapons.

Pfleiderer took deadly aim and shot the Japanese officer before he could see him. Bridwell pulled the trigger on another submariner who moved, and the bullet caught him in the arm. Then there was a hail of bullets into the tree line as the other four sailors began shooting randomly. Pfleiderer picked off one of them and Bridwell another before having to drop to their bellies to avoid the heavy fire. There were only three men left alive, including the wounded one.

As the two U.S. pilots paused to change their clips, they heard what they had feared. One of the Japanese barked an order, and they all jumped up, yelling "banzai," and began charging toward Bridwell and Pfleiderer.

They heard brush rustling as the sailors rushed into the tree line directly at them. Bridwell stood up and shot one point-blank from five feet as the sailor's Arisaka Type 38 rifle released a round over his shoulder, just clipping Bridwell's ear, causing blood to spurt everywhere. Just then, the wounded sailor, who had watched from where the muzzle flash had been, quickly fired three rounds, all embedding in the trunk of a palm tree in front of Bridwell.

Captain Pfleiderer took aim, and with two rounds, the Japanese sailor fell to the beach dead. Bridwell turned to his right and killed the last sailor, who had dropped to his knees to shoot Pfleiderer from his blind side. Bridwell then rushed from the tree line and started pulling the weapons away from the dead men quickly, just in case they were indeed still alive. Pfleiderer followed. With the noise gone and only the crackle of the campfire left, there was an eerie silence.

"Good job, Lieutenant," Pfleiderer said.

"Same to you, Captain," Bridwell replied.

Both men clasped hands, realizing that while they had the edge of surprise, a wild shot from a Japanese weapon could have easily ended their lives. After dragging all of the bodies into the dense foliage, they pulled the black rubber raft next to the P-38 and covered it with palm leaves.

"All of them had submariner badges on. Must have been

in the conning tower and took the emergency ride to the surface. Couldn't have been twenty feet under," Bridwell said.

"Yes, but if they sustained damage to the bulkhead from the rupture in the cruiser, the rest of the crew couldn't have survived," Pfleiderer said.

"I agree. I just hope we're right," Bridwell responded as he dragged the last dead sailor into the bushes.

Once back at the beach, they doused the fire and gathered up the rations and bottles of water.

"Here, take a drink," Pfleiderer said and handed the bottle to Bridwell.

Bridwell took one drink and spit it out.

"Sake," he said.

"Are you kidding? They put rice wine in their survival gear," Pfleiderer said and took a drink. "It's too dry. Dump it out. We don't need something that will make us feel worse. But test each bottle to be sure it's not water."

A few minutes later, they had found five bottles of water out of the eight bottles in the boat and by the campfire.

"Let's collect the weapons and bury them down the beach away from here in case we need them," Bridwell said.

"Good idea," his commanding officer replied.

Once the weapons had been covered with foliage, the two aviators returned to the beach near the now blackened campfire. Sitting down, they began to eat the rations brought ashore by the Japanese submariners.

"The stars are so bright here near the equator. Reminds me of Tucson in the desert," Pfliederer said and took a big gulp of water. He could still taste the salt from the ocean.

"Funny how we both grew up in dry country. You in Arizona, me in Western Oklahoma, and here we are in the middle of the ocean," Bridwell said and took a bite of a cookie of some sort.

"Life gives us strange twists. Just when General MacArthur is about to put the hammer on the Imperial Japanese Army, we are sent out for a routine patrol flight.

So here we sit. If nobody picks up our signal tomorrow, we might just sit out the war here," Pfleiderer said.

"Or longer," Bridwell replied and drank more water.

Laying back on the soft sand of the beach, they both closed their eyes with their last sight being the bright stars of the Southern Cross. Soon they were both asleep, and a few hours later, they were awakened by birds flying overhead as the sun came up. The beach was littered with flotsam and jetsam from the sunken cruiser and submarine. It was mostly just debris from the ship, which was useless to them, but of great curiosity to the birds who were always looking for a free and easy meal.

"We better move inland just in case we get some curious visitors. Let's send one message before the batteries go dead and hope for the best," Pfleiderer said.

They walked toward the army fighter and uncovered it enough to get to the cockpit.

"This is Shark's Leader Two, mayday, mayday. Zero two dash two eight south by one five two dash one one east. Signing out. We'll try it again tomorrow," Pfleiderer said and grabbed a flare gun from inside the cockpit.

"O.K., let's move out," Bridwell said and began following an imaginary trail in the dense foliage.

"I suggest we move toward the high peak in the middle of the island. That would be where the greatest collection of freshwater might be," Pfleiderer proposed.

"I'm right behind you," Bridwell replied and touched the wounded ear that they had bandaged the night before. It throbbed as they walked in the early heat. Their steps created a path through the trees and tropical plants.

"Look ahead. A natural trail," Pfleiderer said.

The two aviators, with Japanese packs on their shoulders holding food and water, walked over to the path that was at least one-meter wide. They gave each other a puzzled look as they took out their guns. Walking more slowly, they were annoyed that the birds of the tropical forest announced their presence with each meter they traveled.

"So much for a stealth approach," Shark's Leader Two said.

"No kidding," Outlaw replied.

Soon the path disappeared, but it was obvious where it had once been, the dense foliage having grown over it again. The elevation of the island path began to climb slowly until they reached a thick growth area and, putting their guns away, started pushing and pulling at the bulky bushes. Suddenly they broke free into a clearing and were startled by the giant stone statue that stood before them.

"Someone used to live here," Bridwell said first.

"From the condition of the path, it's been many years, maybe decades or more," Pfleiderer replied, dropping the heavy pack to the rock surface of the small clearing. The two pilots walked around the giant monolith with a man's face cut into it and then looked around the clearing.

"I remember seeing something like this in a magazine when I was in college," Bridwell said. "It's like one of those big stone faces on Easter Island in the eastern Pacific."

"Maybe Polynesian like we saw when we were stationed at Hickam in Hawaii?" Pfleiderer replied.

"Yeah, maybe, or one of the other groups of native people that used to live on these islands before the war," Bridwell answered back.

Shark's Leader Two, Capt. Pfleiderer, walked around to the back of the giant stone face and stepped back into the dense foliage.

"I've got a hunch," he said as he disappeared into the trees.

Bridwell found a large boulder and sat down. Fifteen minutes passed before Pfleiderer returned to the stone clearing.

"Get your pack and follow me. You won't believe this," he said to Bridwell and stepped back into the brush.

In less than five minutes, they were standing in another clearing at the base of the tallest peak on the island, an ancient volcano. A small freshwater stream ran through the middle of the clearing. The clearing was decorated with more monoliths and carvings on the face of the rocky cliff in front of them.

"Must have been a ceremonial circle of some kind," Bridwell noted.

"Take a look at this," Pfleiderer said from the side of the clearing.

Bridwell walked over and stood next to him where there was a small opening in the trees. The two were awed that they had been climbing up the hidden trail and were now looking out across the beautiful blue lagoon from nearly five hundred feet above the beach.

"No wonder I'm tired," Bridwell said.

"Me too. We began climbing the minute we left the beach," Pfleiderer said.

"Yes, sir, Captain," Bridwell replied and saluted.

They quickly filled their water containers and drank too much too fast, causing them to sprawl out on the ground. Suddenly the noise of an aircraft flying over the lagoon could be heard, and the two men gave each other a startled look. They stood up just in time to see a U.S. Navy PBY Catalina flying five hundred feet over the lagoon.

"They made our radio message," Pfleiderer announced as he hurriedly took the flare gun from the Japanese pack.

With a sharp aim, he fired it through the opening just as the PBY made another pass over the lagoon. The pilot of the navy rescue aircraft tilted his wings back and forth, in acknowledgment that he had seen the flare. After one more pass, the big grey PBY began to settle down on the smooth surface of the lagoon, awaiting its passengers to appear on the beach.

Halfway down the mountain, Pfleiderer fired another flare to show their progress.

"Captain, they're almost to the beach," a sailor said from the back of the PBY.

"Break out the raft and go get them and hurry. We have to assume a nearby Japanese aircraft or ship may have detected our arrival. Be quick," he ordered.

"Aye, Captain," the sailor responded.

By the time the PBY's raft touched the beach, the two pilots were running out of the tropical tree line toward them, their packs still hung over their shoulders. Once they arrived at the raft, they tossed in their packs.

"We're glad to see you guys," Shark's Leader Two said to the sailors.

Soon the raft was next to the open side door of the PBY, and the pilots and the sailors were all inside.

"Welcome aboard soldiers," the PBY pilot said.

"Thanks Captain, good to be aboard," Outlaw replied.

The two aviators looked at each other and then grasped hands and smiled. They knew they had lived to fight and face death another day.

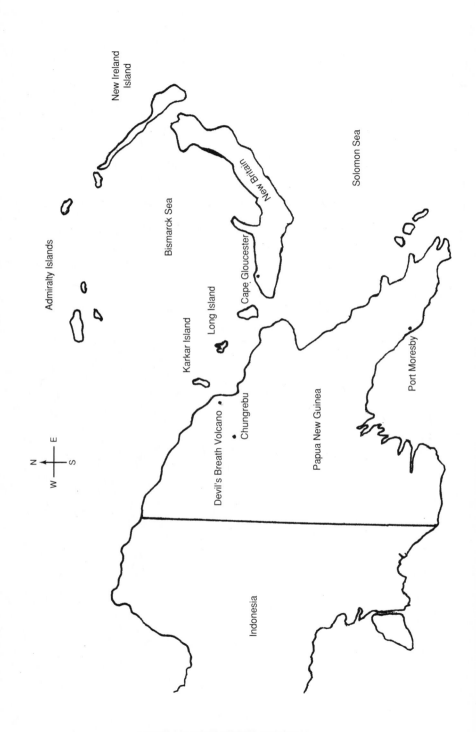

1

Gwennie and Kitty Koo
Southwest of New Britain Island, January 2001

Chris MacGregor held on tightly to the wheel of the Cessna Caravan as the winds buffeted it up and down.

"Where'd this storm come from?" Natalie asked as she peered through her side window at the shadows of what appeared to be an island chain below.

"I don't know," Chris replied. "All the weather reports said we'd have clear skies with patchy showers."

"Doesn't look patchy to me," Heather added from the seat behind Natalie.

"It looks like it's going to break just ahead," Chris said as the rain continued to lash across the windshield of the amphibian. "The radar says we're only ten miles from the island. At this speed we'll be over it in six minutes."

"Are we going to miss it?" R.O. asked from behind Chris.

"No, everyone relax. It's just a tropical rain shower. The Aussies taught me how to find atolls like this last week while I was at Cairn," Chris said.

"I bet that training camp was fun," Natalie said, showing her confidence in Chris.

"It was twenty-one days of the most interesting camp

25

I've ever attended. I was so glad Dad got me into it. Just to
think that I got to eat, sleep, dive, fly, and parachute with
the Royal Australian Navy Seals was just awesome," Chris
said and adjusted the course of the plane slightly.

"I can't remember who you said was there," R.O. said,
leaning toward him.

"Just guys and girls my age from across Australia. They
all had some connection, like a family member in the mili-
tary or government, and had an interest in diving or flying.
I was the only American, but the fact that Mom is a British
subject as well as an American citizen qualified me. You
know the Commonwealth thing and all that stuff about the
Queen makes us half-British in their eyes. There were a few
of us who wanted to fly and dive. But I think jumping out
of a helicopter at two thousand feet in diving gear and
parachuting into the ocean was the most exciting," Chris
described with a big grin on his face.

"More exciting than this? Flying in a tropical storm?"
Heather asked in a worried tone.

"Sure, but this is fun too," he replied.

"Didn't we read about Amelia Earhart getting lost trying
to find an island?" Heather asked.

"Yea and she was never found," R.O. added. "Some say
the Japs got her."

"That's Japanese, Ryan," Natalie corrected. "It's rude to
use words like that."

"That's what they called them in World War II," R.O.
shot back.

"This isn't World War II, Ryan. So cool it," Heather
added.

"Aviation is much more sophisticated now anyway,"
Chris retorted.

"Yea, but she flew around the world," R.O. said.

"You guys are making me nervous," Natalie added.
"And Chris did fly us across China without a problem."

"There she is," Chris said and pointed out the front

window. "Just as the map and the satellite said, due west of Cape Gloucester and north of Umboi Island. It's a small atoll called Tolokiwa where the Japanese destroyer *Arashio* was sunk during World War II in 1943."

"Was there a big battle there?" R.O. asked.

"Yes, it was the Battle of the Bismarck Sea with both submarine and air attack. It sits just adjacent to the shallow lagoon. The dive master at the hotel said it was a good dive," Chris replied.

The rain stopped and sunlight pierced through the clouds as Chris began a sharp descent. He flew the Cessna Caravan amphibian parallel to the coral reef in the lagoon and dropped down to one thousand feet. The skies opened up and sunlight filled the lagoon, revealing the crystal-clear water, which reflected a bright turquoise color against the white beach and lush green foliage. As the pontoons touched down gently, barely a splash was left in the wake. The daily flying time in Australia had helped polish Chris's aviator skills.

The aircraft glided across the lagoon as if it were an elegant black-browed mollymawk albatross coming in for a landing.

"Where's the dive spot?" R.O. asked and stared out the window.

"The map said that it's on the edge of the lagoon, northeast end," Chris replied. "Natalie, get out the map and we'll anchor the plane near the beach on that end of the lagoon."

"Now remind me how you found out about this wreck and why Mom let us do this," Heather said. "I really did forget."

"I found out about the wreck from the divemaster at the Royal Australian Navy Seal camp. I had told him Dad was going to be involved in the reef management project near Papua New Guinea and Mom wanted to spend two weeks vacationing in the islands. That's when he said we should visit this sunken Japanese destroyer from World War II and then go on to the Solomons to see all the ships there," Chris answered patiently as he drove the plane across the glass smooth surface of the lagoon.

"I remember," Heather said unconvincingly. "But that still doesn't explain the parent thing; you know, how you got permission to do this."

"I think Chris proved himself in China," Natalie responded and turned around to Heather and smiled.

"I agree. I just couldn't remember," Heather said giving up on the argument and turning to the window.

Just a few minutes later, the Cessna Caravan was resting still on the water and Chris was dropping a sea anchor down to the white sandy bottom ten feet below just missing a passing school of fish. Heather stood at the door, dove into the warm water, and swam the one hundred feet to the beach. Chris inflated a small rubber boat and started loading diving gear into it.

"You do such good work," Natalie said as she dropped her T-shirt in the cabin, revealing a tropical print bikini. She dove into the water and swam toward the beach.

"Yea, you do," R.O. said and tried to step by Chris.

"Hold it, buddy. You're staying with me," Chris said and grabbed the back of his T-shirt.

"That's not fair," R.O. whined.

"You've got to be quicker and slyer like the girls," Chris suggested and handed him a dive bag. "I'll get the tanks, you get the gear."'

"Alright," R.O. said and tossed more equipment into the yellow rubber boat.

It wasn't long before all four kids were on the beach with dive equipment laid out and ready to go. Each one put on their equipment without any help, and Chris stepped out into the small surf of the lagoon with a pair of fins in his left hand and a goody bag in his right hand. He had on a one-millimeter wet suit and twelve pounds of weights. A Nikon® camera dangled from his neck. Each teen had a knife on their right or left leg and a utility belt that held a flashlight and tools for cutting wire and any other object that they might get tangled into. All had one tank, and Chris left two extra tanks on the beach.

"Everyone ready?" Chris asked into his new radio-equipped mask and looked around.

"Ready when you are," Natalie answered. "No hurricanes or sharks like the last two times I went diving with you." She smiled.

R.O. walked out into the water, put his mask on and sat down to slip on his fins. Heather was last, and soon all four were in ten feet of water and swimming under the airplane. In another one hundred yards, they were leaving the calm part of the lagoon and approaching the reef. Looming in the shadows of the reef was the sunken Japanese warship. The water was crystal clear with visibility to two hundred feet. The temperature was almost eighty degrees.

Beautiful reef fishes swam everywhere. The menagerie of shapes and colors were like an underwater carnival that allowed one's eyes to feast upon nature's beauty. Curious butterfly fish swam up to the teens and schooled along side for a few minutes before darting back to the safety of the reef. A small ray shot across the bottom flapping its pectoral fins like wings in search of a mollusk for a quick meal.

As the kids approached from the starboard side of the Japanese ship, they noticed the cruiser's guns pointed majestically toward the open sea. The tower was only ten feet from the surface with the main deck at fifty feet. Chris had already instructed everyone that this would be a "jump" dive with no decompression other than two minutes at fifteen feet. That meant when they reached the main deck, they had twenty minutes before it was time to come back up. R.O. had received a strong five minutes of instruction from his father, Dr. Jack MacGregor, before they had left Cape Gloucester. There had been no threats of going back to the States and missing the rest of the year-long trip around the world; that tactic didn't work any more. It had been a simple ultimatum any thirteen year old would understand—behave or your life would become miserable very soon.

The divers moved through the broken opening in the reef where the cruiser had sunk over sixty years ago and were headed down to the main deck at a leisurely kick. The reef had begun to repair itself with new coral everywhere and colorful sponges and tubeworms making a new home on the surface of the ship. From that distance, they could see the hole in the side of the ship that had been made by an American torpedo during a fierce battle.

The hole was grown over with a variety of soft corals and marine life. Anemones had attached to the jagged edges, and orange-and-white-striped clown fish darted in and out of the hole, trying to lure smaller fish into the stinging arms of the anemone that waved in the current.

Suddenly a fifty-pound grouper emerged from the hole, swimming right up to Chris's face and stopping. Its big lips were all puffed out and slowly opening and closing as if it were talking to him. Chris gently reached out and petted him. The big spotted grouper then moved to the side and let him swim closer to the ship. The big fish never left his side for the entire dive as if telling everyone that this was his ship, his home.

"Is everyone O.K.?" Chris asked into the microphone in his mask.

After a response from everyone, he continued to lead them to the Imperial Japanese Navy ship *Arashio Maru*. Heather was just behind him with R.O. at her side. Natalie pulled up the rear and glanced at her depth gauge; it read forty-five feet. Her dive computer on her wrist told her she had fifty-two minutes at depth before decompression would have to begin. Chris looked her way, and she gave him a hand sign to check his dive computer, forgetting that she could talk to him. He did and waved back.

"Use your microphone. Did you forget?" Chris asked.

"Yes, I am so not used to having it," Heather replied.

"I'm not. I love telling everyone about what I find," R.O. chimed in.

"You guys are so spoiled," Natalie said and waved to Chris.

They were approaching the main deck of the warship, and the big guns loomed in their faces. Attached to the main deck was a catapult loaded with a Mitsubishi AGM2 fighter, also known as the Zero. As the kids swam closer, they could see that it was draped with an assortment of marine organisms, ranging from tubeworms to exotic sponges.

R.O. reached out and touched the gill extension of one of the worms, and it retracted instantly into its cavernous and protected covering. Chris shook his finger back and forth as if to tell R.O. "No." All the kids wore protective diving gloves. They were experienced divers knowing that the sea is the home of hundreds of animals whose natural protective devices can be toxic to humans. A simple touch could lead to a swollen hand the size of a head of cabbage.

"Heads up everybody. We've got twenty minutes left at fifty feet," Chris said into his radio microphone-equipped mask." He then followed with a hand signal to everyone just to be sure he was understood. Everyone responded with an O.K. and continued along the war-torn deck, pockmarked with holes from American aircraft trying to sink the mighty destroyer before a deadly torpedo found its mark.

As Natalie passed by an open door, another large grouper lunged out and startled her. She let out a muffled scream. Everyone else smiled. Chris entered the main part of the ship just below the tower and found himself inside the radar room, which had equipment that was considered beyond its time in 1944. R.O. swam in behind him and stayed about five feet from Chris's yellow fins. Chris stopped next to a hatch that looked like it had been pried open recently with a tool of some sort. He pointed to the scratches and tool marks on the edge of the door. Pulling it open a little more, he looked inside and turned on his flashlight. R.O. did the same, and the room was illuminated instantly.

From the size of the compartment and the location next to the communications center, Chris guessed that it might be the captain's quarters. He swam through the opening and into the large room where he saw that the invertebrate life, which had grown on the surface of the tables, cabinets, and metal furniture, had been disturbed as if someone had been looking for something. The big grouper followed behind R.O.

"I think I'll name you," R.O. said.

"Natalie, Heather, check in," Chris spoke.

"We're good," Natalie replied. "Just checking out the airplane on the deck. Where are you?"

"We're just under the tower. There's an open hatch door. Follow it in here. We've got ten minutes left," Chris answered back.

He then turned and saw R.O. with his knife out, poking into the remainder of a cabinet on the far wall.

"What is it?" Chris asked.

"Just a tunnel of some kind. I saw a black-and-orange fish swim into the hole, and I was just looking to see how deep it went," R.O. replied.

"Let me help." Chris got out his long multipurpose tool and wedged it against the edge of what looked like a shelf of some kind.

A beautiful Achilles Tang, also known as an orange doctor fish, instantly swam out. Its black, sleek body was accented with a false orange eye seemingly painted next to its tail to distract a predator into charging toward it's tail fin, allowing the fish to escape in the opposite direction.

"That's it," R.O. said. "Really cool, huh?"

"Yea, Dad would love to see that specimen," Chris replied.

Chris kept pushing and suddenly the metal cabinet began to move; then the wall began to move.

"Watch out," Chris yelled into his microphone.

The entire wall fell forward, kicking up sixty years of silt and debris. Both boys froze as they were suddenly in a very dark room with only about a foot of visibility. After waiting for the water to partially clear, Chris swam back toward where the wall had been and was confronted with the front door of a safe.

"My gosh. Look at this R.O.," he said just as his dive computer began to beep and tell him it was time to ascend to fifteen feet.

"A safe. Let's open it," R.O. said excitedly.

"We don't have the tools or the air. Girls, head to the rendezvous point above the bow of the ship. We'll ascend together. We'll change tanks and come back for the safe," he said and winked at R.O.

"What safe?" Natalie responded.

"Yes!" R.O. said and turned toward the door in the silt-laden room.

Within minutes, everyone was suspended weightlessly above the bow and headed for a brief decompression stop at fifteen feet. It was just a precaution to get all the small bubbles out of the bloodstream. R.O. couldn't stop talking the entire two minutes about how he had once again discovered a treasure.

"It probably has nothing in it but the silt left from decayed papers and paper money," Chris said.

"Who knows, Chris, there might be some gold coins in there," Natalie said, fueling R.O.'s excitement.

"Well, whatever is in there was being sought by some other diver who pretty much tore up the skeleton of the room looking for it. We just got lucky and pried in the right spot and brought the whole wall down," Chris replied and pointed up for everyone to surface.

Like a school of fish, the four teens slowly rose to the surface and then put their snorkels in their mouths for the short swim to the beach. Just as they reached the beach a de Havilland Beaver buzzed them, not fifty feet in the air. They recognized the plane as the same model belonging to Jessica

Gailey in Alaska, but this one was painted canary yellow.

As they stood up out of the water and took off their equipment, Chris looked up in the sky as the de Havilland lined up to land in the lagoon next to them.

"I sure hope those aren't the people who were looking for that safe," he said.

"Me too," Natalie agreed as she walked over next to him, wringing the water out of her hair.

The amphibian cruised smoothly across the waves, touched down without a bounce, and then powered across the water toward them.

"I'm scared," Heather said softly.

"Well, everyone get ready to swim to the plane when I say go," Chris said, tensing up.

The yellow amphibian came to a stop about ten feet from the beach with its pontoons lightly digging into the sand. The propeller wound down, and the door flew open. To their surprise, a reddish-yellow cat jumped from the inside of the airplane and landed in about a foot of water. It quickly swam to the beach and shook off; then it turned toward the kids and gave them a big meow.

"What on earth?" Natalie asked.

"That's Kitty Koo, and she's telling you that she's hungry," shouted a gray-haired old woman now standing on the pontoon.

The teens stood with their mouths wide open, realizing that this elderly woman had just landed the amphibian in the lagoon. She turned back to the airplane and pulled out an already loaded pneumatic spear gun. The kids stepped back. She pointed down toward the water, took aim, and pulled the trigger.

"Dinner's coming, Kitty Koo," she said and reeled in the line with a ten-inch fish on the end of the spear. She then stepped down into the knee-deep water and walked up to the beach. Taking a knife from her belt, she quickly lopped off the head of the fish and cut out its organs. In one smooth motion, she tossed the fish to the cat, who immediately began to tear into the flesh.

The kids were dumbfounded and speechless.

"My name's Gwendolyn. My friends call me Gwennie. What are you kids doing out here?" the old woman asked.

"Just diving on the wreck," Chris responded.

"I work for the Papua New Guinea Department of Historical Preservation, and I need to see your permit," Gwennie said.

"We didn't know we needed a permit," Chris answered back.

"Young man, just because we're hundreds of miles from anywhere you'd reckon to be civilized doesn't mean you can come in here and act like you own the place. If you don't have a permit, then I'll have to issue you a warning. Next time it will be a five hundred dollar fine," she said. "I can also sell you a permit for one hundred dollars."

"One hundred dollars!" Heather exclaimed.

"Yep, that's a whole lot cheaper than the fine. And if you had brought up anything from that Japanese ship, then I'd have to fine you and call for someone to come arrest you," she said.

"Arrest us?" Natalie asked.

"That's right. You kids have hearing problems?" she replied.

"We're good," Chris said, "And thanks for the warning. I'll get my billfold out of the airplane and pay you."

"Kitty Koo, want another fish?" the old woman said and walked up the beach to a fallen tree and sat down. The reddish-yellow cat ran up to her with the remains of the fish in its mouth and rubbed up against the elderly woman's wet pant leg. The kids walked over as Chris swam out to the airplane to get the money for the permit. Within a few minutes, he was back, dripping from the swim. He handed her a wet one hundred dollar bill.

"Do you have any identification so we know that

you're not just taking our money?" Natalie asked.

"Honey, I've got all the identification I need right here," Gwennie said and took off her straw hat.

She reached inside the crown, pulled out a laminated piece of paper about the size of a credit card, and handed it to Natalie. Natalie looked at it and handed it to Chris who perused it carefully.

"Well, you are who you say you are Gwendolyn Zorger. This says you live in Cape Gloucester. That's a long flight out here," Chris said, handing her card back to her.

"This is the farthest I fly. I normally don't come out this way but once a month, but we've had reports from the locals on these islands of some suspicious boats and aircraft over the last couple of months. There are five of us flying this area; I just happened to see that bright red Caravan floating out there and thought I would drop in for a visit," she said.

"What if we had been some bad guys?" Heather asked with a smile.

The old woman reached behind her bulky khaki shirt and produced a Taurus 9mm-automatic pistol.

"She's small but she makes a loud bang and a sharp sting if I need her. With these seventy-two-year-old blue eyes I can shoot an eye out of a coconut at fifty feet," she said.

"Cool," R.O. chimed in.

"But I could see you were a bunch of kids so I wasn't afraid to come down," she said as she put the gun away. "Besides, Kitty Koo was hungry, and we wouldn't be stopping for another hour to refuel before flying back to Cape Gloucester tonight," she said.

"That's where we're staying. We just got there yesterday, and my friend, Chris, couldn't wait to come out here and dive," Natalie said.

"Is there a good place to eat when we get back?" Heather asked. "I'm sure I'll be hungry by then. In fact, I'm hungry right now."

"That's a ditto from me," R.O added as he petted the

cat and took the fish spine from its mouth gently.

"Billy Fly's. Best island food around," Gwennie replied.

"Billy Fly's? What's that?" R.O. asked.

"Billy's an old friend who's been around here for about twenty years. He and his pal Bill Hill, whom everybody calls by his Indian name, Young Deer, own the restaurant and pub on the beach. Great food," Gwendolyn said.

"Billy and Bill. I knew two women named Ginna and Regina," R.O. said.

"Don't go there again," Heather said, showing her annoyance with her little brother.

"Can you get them confused?" Chris asked.

"Nope. Billy Fly is the old guy with a tan like a lizard and white hair down to his shoulders. Young Deer is the young guy, I think Cherokee or something like that. He's got long black hair and is about six foot two. Come here Kitty Koo," Gwennie said. The cat jumped into her lap. "Time to go. Here's your money back young man. I'm going to give you a break this time. Tell your folks to buy a permit next time," she said and handed him the one hundred dollar bill back.

"Well, I guess we've all been rude," Natalie said. "We didn't introduce ourselves."

"You're Chris MacGregor, and these two are your brother and sister, Ryan and Heather, and you must be Natalie Crosswhite," Gwennie said.

The kids stared at her in amazement.

"The numbers on the airplane checked out I guess," Chris said.

"Yes, son, they did, and your mother said for the four of you to high tail it back to the resort pronto," Gwennie replied.

"Mom. Is there no place on this planet we can escape her?" Heather said and rolled her eyes.

"Moms know everything, see everything, and well, you know," Gwennie said as she waded back to the de Havilland with Kitty Koo under one arm and her spear gun under the other. "Don't just stand there, come give me a push out of the sand," she barked at the kids.

Within a few moments, the amphibian aircraft was floating free and the spry old woman had the airplane fired up and turning slightly in the surf until she was pointed out toward the long end of the lagoon. Five minutes later, she was climbing to five thousand feet and heading back toward Cape Gloucester on the island of New Britain. Kitty Koo, her belly full of fresh fish, was curled up in the passenger seat already asleep.

While in the deep below awaited the secrets of the safe long ago forgotten or so they thought.

2

The Arashio Maru

―――――――――◯▭◯――――――――――

"That was amazing," Natalie said as they all watched the yellow plane climb into the clouds.

"Can we swim back to the wreck and get the safe?" R.O. asked, immediately turning the attention back to the mystery at hand.

Chris thought for a moment, walking around on the sand and looking out to the sea. "Well, we don't have a permit, and she said we're not allowed to take anything from the destroyer," Chris said.

"Yea, but those other guys are going to come back and get the safe," R.O. pleaded.

"He's right, Chris," Natalie said. "If there is something valuable in it, then it would be lost forever. If we got it, then we could turn it in."

"Or keep it if it is lost treasure and be millionaires," R.O. added excitedly.

"I'm for getting it," Heather said.

"O.K., I've got two more tanks of air and that should do it," Chris said reluctantly. "Natalie, I want you and Heather to inflate the raft and position it right over the wreck. Fins,

snorkels, and snorkel vests are all you need. Take your
knives too. We're going to have to tie onto the safe and then
drag it across the bottom of the lagoon. I don't think we'll
be able to lift it without a winch. But I can tie it to a pontoon
of the plane and then pull it to the beach. The four of us
should be able to carry it in from shallow water."

Chris and R.O. swam back to the plane and opened the
side hatch. Changing out their regulators from the spent
tanks to the new ones took only seconds. Within minutes,
they were geared up and swimming toward the wreck on
the surface to conserve air. Chris held a yellow nylon rope
in his left hand. R.O. was at his right side. When they had
reached the area just above the *Arashio Maru,* they put their
snorkels to the side and tightened the straps on the new
masks. Chris gave a thumbs-up to R.O. who did the same
right back. He then remembered he could talk underwater
with the new equipment.

"Ready to go down?" Chris asked into the microphone.

"Roger," R.O. replied.

As if they were synchronized swimmers, both flipped
over, fins coming out of the water and going head down in
the blue lagoon. The water was so clear they appeared to be
floating in air. The Japanese destroyer loomed ahead in the
shallow lagoon as if it were a giant monolith of the sea
gods. To R.O., it seemed to be a toy ship waiting for him to
explore even more. The descent took five minutes as they
easily kicked, trying to save their energy for the heavy
work ahead. R.O. had to stop twice and equalize his ears
but soon caught up with Chris.

As they approached the main deck, Chris checked his
dive computer and was comfortable with the readings. The
big grouper came out to meet them again. Chris surmised
they had plenty of time to get into the captain's cabin, tie
onto the safe, and drag it out to the main deck. As they
passed by the Zero, a barracuda swam by. R.O. almost
believed that it was smiling when it showed him its long

needlelike teeth. Within two more minutes, they were back in the cabin and swam directly to the wall where the safe was nestled. The silt had settled, and the visibility was clear all across the cabin.

Chris rubbed the silt off the small safe and put his hands behind it, testing its weight. It moved a couple of inches.

"I think we can do this," Chris said. "Move over to my right, and when I say 'Go,' pull forward. Don't forget, there's a three foot drop to the floor so keep your feet and legs out of the way."

"Gotcha," R.O. said, positioning himself to the side and grabbing the safe with his gloved hands.

"Ready. Set. Go!" Chris spoke into the microphone.

The two MacGregor boys pulled, and the safe fell forward quickly, surprising both of them. It lunged from its sixty-year-old hole in the wall and dropped to the floor of the cabin. Silt jumped up from the floor like a miniature volcano blowing ash into the atmosphere.

"Wow, that's incredible," R.O. said.

"Ditto that," Chris replied. "The only explanation for it moving so easily is that it still must be air tight and the bubble inside is helping us with the mass of the safe. At least that's what I'm hoping."

The silt began to settle as Chris and R.O. leaned down and together lifted the safe off the floor.

"It's heavy, but we can handle it. Don't stop until we get to the deck," Chris said as they shuffled their fins in the debris of the fallen wall. After ten minutes of work, they were on the deck still holding on to the safe.

"Set it down," Chris said and looked up at the rope dangling down to them from the bright yellow raft.

They could see Heather with her masked face in the water looking down at them.

"Let's tie the rope around the safe like a net, and then we'll attach it to the line to the raft," Chris instructed.

Soon the old safe was wrapped up tight and Chris had

attached the two clamps from the rope suspended from the raft.

"O.K. Let's move the safe over to the edge of the deck. Be careful not to let it fall off the deck. That's a ninety-foot plunge to the bottom; we don't have enough air or rope to get it back, and this might pull down the raft. Whoever was here before us today will be back, and it will be easy pickings for them to extract it from the lagoon," Chris said.

"Gotcha," R.O. said, and they began to drag the safe to the edge of the deck. Stopping just two feet from the side, R.O. peered over the edge about the time a school of venomous Striped catfish swam by them.

"Wow, look at those," he said. "Are those the dangerous fish on the chart you got at the hotel?"

"I think so. Stay away just in case they are. My dive computer says that it's time to go up," Chris said and pointed to the computer on his right wrist. "Follow your smallest bubble to the top. Let's go."

Chris and R.O. gave a small kick and held onto the rope as they left the Japanese ship and headed to the top. Looking back down, they could see the safe perched on the edge of the deck. Once they reached fifteen feet, they stopped; Chris looked at his Rolex Submariner and timed the two minutes they needed to stay for a short decompression. Then Chris pointed up, and they emerged next to the raft.

"Did you get it?" Heather shouted over the nearby noise of the waves crashing over the reef at the edge of the lagoon.

"Sure did. I always get my treasure," R.O. called back as he took his mask off.

"I'll swim ashore and get the plane. You guys stay here and secure the rope," Chris said as he began to kick toward the plane.

It was fifteen minutes before he could dump his gear in the rear baggage area of the Cessna and pull up the anchor.

He fired up the engine and drove it across the water toward the yellow raft. The closer he got to the breakers at the reef, the more the plane bounced up and down. He made a tight circle around the raft and drove the left wing over the top of it, safely keeping the prop away from Natalie, Heather, and R.O.

He pointed down to the pontoon. R.O. got the message, swam over to it and began to tie the rope around the large float, which doubled as a landing gear. Chris watched from the window and gave him a thumbs-up when the knot was secure. He then waved them away from the plane as he powered it up and started to move away from the wreck. The line grew taught as the safe began to slide in the silt on the deck of the destroyer. Suddenly it fell free of the old ship and swung into the open ocean of the lagoon.

Chris felt a tug on the port side of the plane and increased power. He knew that the safe would hit the bottom slope of the lagoon in about a hundred yards. He kept the power steady and pointed the plane toward the beach. Before long, he felt the drag of the safe as it dug into the sandy bottom. He kept the plane lined up straight with two tall trees on the beach so he wouldn't tear up any coral or other marine life. Chris had surveyed the bottom earlier as he and R.O. swam out to the wreck. The rope was fifty feet long so when the pontoons rested on the beach the safe would be in six feet of water. He thought that would be good enough to pull to shore.

He looked over his shoulder out the window and saw the girls paddling the yellow raft behind him and R.O., kicking along on the surface. After a few more seconds, he felt the pontoons hit the bottom and stick. He turned off the power, and the prop twirled to a stop. Anxiously, he climbed out of the seat and onto the pontoon. Still in his wet suit, he jumped into the water, grabbed the tight rope, and followed it with his gloved hands fifty feet to the safe.

"Still there," he yelled as the raft approached with the

girls asking questions he couldn't hear. R.O. was about twenty feet behind them as they tossed their two paddles in the bottom of the raft and climbed out to drop into the lagoon. Both went in over their heads and bobbed back to the surface.

"Hey! It's too deep here," Heather said as she spit out seawater.

"Just grab the rope and swim ten more feet and your head will be out of the water," Chris responded.

Natalie just winked at him. "Good job," she said as she swam by.

When R.O. arrived, Chris began to bark out orders.

"Keep your mask on, and we'll go down and drag the safe ten feet to the girls. Then we'll carry it to the beach," he said.

"Got it," R.O. responded and lowered himself to the bottom. Chris slipped on the small face mask he had taken out of his bag and took a deep breath. He dropped down beside R.O., and together they began to drag the safe across the bottom. Chris had to surface twice to get a breath of air as the work spent his oxygen quickly. R.O. was still using his diving gear.

Before he knew it, extra gloved hands were reaching for the roped harness of the safe as Natalie and Heather joined in the labor. Before long, they were steadily moving the safe across the shallows of the lagoon and onto the beach. When the safe was out of the water, all four collapsed on the sand and didn't say a word.

"I hereby claim this Japanese treasure as property of Ryan O'Keefe MacGregor, treasure finder incorporated. If y'all are nice, I'll split it with you," R.O. said as he got up, walked over, and sat on the small safe.

"Ryan, shut up," Heather said and sat up.

Natalie was next up and walked over to the safe.

"That's pretty small to hold much treasure. Why wasn't it heavier than it was?" she asked.

"I think it has an air bubble in it. It seems to be air tight and should have been much heavier in the water than it was considering the effort it took to set it on the beach," Chris replied. "O.K., let's put it in the plane and get out of here before the cat lady comes back or the looters who were here before us show up."

"I've changed my mind. Doesn't this make us looters?" Heather asked.

Everyone grew quiet and looked at Chris. He stood silent for a minute.

"No. We're salvagers because whatever we find of value we will turn over to the authorities. We've already discussed this so it's a dead issue," he said.

"Wait a minute, if there's treasure in there, I get to keep some of it," R.O. said with an angry look on his face.

"Most countries have salvager's rights, and if, and I mean a big if, there was something of value in there, then we would get a share of it. The point is we don't break the law. We report it," Chris said. "Now let's get moving. It's three o'clock, and Mom will be waiting for us at the resort."

The four teens again picked up the safe and carried it over to the side door of the Caravan where they gently set it in. Chris tied it down to protect the plane in case they hit any turbulence. Thirty minutes later, they had the raft deflated and stowed away with all of their diving gear. Hot, wet, and with sea salt in their hair and on their skin, they welcomed the air conditioner of the airplane as Chris taxied down the lagoon to face the oncoming breeze from the ocean.

"Chris, we've got company," Natalie said pointing toward a black twin-engine de Havilland Otter descending into the lagoon.

"Buckle up tight, it's going to be a game of chicken," Chris said, pushing the throttle forward.

"I'm ready," hollered R.O. from the back seat next to Heather.

Heather tightened her belt and finished putting her hair in a ponytail with a pink scrunchy.

"I'm ready," she said.

Chris pointed the amphibian directly up the middle of the lagoon toward the landing aircraft that was occupying the center lane, so to speak.

"Those could be the guys who were going through the captain's cabin but didn't find the secret wall," Chris said.

"I did," R.O. added, unnecessarily reminding them all.

"You're annoying. This is serious business," Heather shot back to R.O.

Chris's Caravan gained speed, closing quickly on the approaching aircraft. He could feel the lift under the wings pull at the surface tension of the ocean, waiting for the pontoons to lift into the sky. The other airplane moved closer and closer. Then suddenly the pontoons broke free, and the drag ceased to pull back on the speed of the plane.

"We're up," Chris said.

"They're getting closer," Natalie warned.

Heather closed her eyes.

"Pull up Chris," R.O. shouted over the noise.

Without much effort, the Cessna Caravan lifted high in the air, and Chris banked it toward the beach, continuing to climb as the other amphibian increased its throttle but didn't have enough distance at the end of the lagoon to take off. It would have to turn around and take off into the wind as Chris had.

Chris then banked the plane toward the high peak of the island and out to sea. The thirty-minute flight back to New Britain would pass quickly. The three passengers had fallen asleep by the time Chris reached five thousand feet. He set the course to their new temporary home on this sixth leg of their adventure around the globe. The black de Havilland Otter didn't follow them. Chris was still puzzled; what could be of such great importance in the small safe of a ship that was sunk over sixty years ago. What he couldn't foretell were the events of the next few days that would make that mystery become insignificant to their lives.

3

Cape Gloucester

As the Cessna Caravan taxied across the man-made lagoon next to the airport, the girls and R.O. awoke from their short nap. Coming to a stop next to a pier, a dock-worker jogged over and tied up the pontoons next to the plane rental business where Chris had acquired the Cessna.

"What about the safe?" Natalie asked.

"Take my large dive bag and cut it open so it can slide over the top of it," Chris replied.

R.O. climbed over the second seat, took out a diving knife, and began to cut the bag, tossing the contents next to the other dive bags. Once he made the cut big enough, he slid it over the rope harness that was still around the safe. One of the dock men opened the side door just as R.O. finished covering the safe.

"Did you have a good dive today?" he asked in English with his heavy island accent.

"Yeah, it was great," R.O. responded and stepped out.

"Go get us a cab," Chris said quickly to Natalie.

"You got it," she replied and hurried down the dock to the office.

R.O. and Chris picked up the bag holding the camouflaged safe and began to move as quickly as they could
down the dock, grunting all the way. By the time they
reached the street next to the office, they were rolling with
sweat in the tropical heat. Heather was behind them dragging one dive bag and carrying a second one. Natalie
walked up to them from the other direction.

"See if we left anything in the plane," Chris said as she
approached.

Without saying a word, she ran back down the dock just
as the dockhand was unloading the dive tanks.

"All empty. Must have had a good day," the man commented.

"We did. It was fun," Natalie replied

"Don't worry about anything else. I'll take care of the
tanks and refuel the plane. It's all part of the price of the
daily rental," the man said.

"Thanks so much," Natalie said, grabbing her bag and
the two maps that Chris had brought. She then turned and
picked up his sunglasses from the console and put them in
her hair. She looked in the back seat and noticed a hairbrush that had fallen to the floor and grabbed that.

"You guys don't need a mother when I'm around," she
whispered under her breath.

"Did you say something, Miss?" the man asked as he
returned from carrying two air tanks over to a compressor
station.

"I said I just found my hairbrush." She showed it to him
and smiled, still nervous about the safe.

"We are going to get into so much trouble," she thought
to herself as she hurried up the dock. "Mavis will put me on
a plane to Oklahoma so fast."

As she reached the others, a van from the hotel resort
pulled to a stop and a man hopped out to help with the
gear. He reached for the bag that covered the safe and R.O.
quickly sat on it.

"I think I have a rock in my flip-flop," R.O. explained.

The man just looked at him and grabbed another dive bag instead. Chris turned and, with Heather and R.O., picked up the safe and set it inside the van and immediately piled stuff on top of it.

As he walked around the van, the driver asked, "Heavy bag?"

"Diving weights," R.O. answered quickly.

"Now we're lying," Natalie mumbled to herself. "It gets deeper."

The van moved along the coast road down a shady lane of coconut trees. With the resort complex a short ride away, the kids rode quietly. The minute the van stopped, Chris hopped out and grabbed a luggage carrier from the grip of a bellhop.

"O.K. guys, I'll tip the driver; you get the stuff loaded," Chris said. He distracted the driver while they moved the safe to the luggage carrier and piled their diving gear on it again. The four then pushed the brass carrier through the sliding glass doors and were welcomed with a blast of cold air from the lobby. Goose bumps formed all over their arms, and their skin tightened. Just as they turned the corner toward the elevators, a tall brunette in blue shorts and a white top stopped in front of them.

"Hi, Mom," Heather said suddenly.

The others just stood there with eyes wide-open and sucking air.

"Well, that's a nice greeting. How was your day trip? Did that nice lady with the cat find you and deliver my message?" She asked. There was a long pause.

"Hello! Does anyone speak English?" she commented with her hands on her hips.

"Mom, we're great," Chris replied.

"Had scads of fun diving," Natalie said.

"Scads, did you? That must mean you had a great day. A little sunburn maybe. Didn't anyone wear sun block? Well no, it doesn't look like it," Mavis said, examining each one carefully. "We moved our rooms to the bungalows down by the beach. I was just checking to see if we had left anything in the suite. It's bungalow number 14 on the path out that door. And rinse down your diving gear. You might want to use it again while we're here. There's an outdoor shower just for that purpose. It's 4:00 now; we're going to eat at 6:00 at the restaurant on the beach. A place called Billy Fly's, at least that's what I think it is or something like that."

"Heather and Natalie are in hut 15, and you boys are in 16. Number 14 is the big one with the den and kitchen. Your dad is lingering down there somewhere. One of his marine biology buddies just flew in, and they're meeting tomorrow about some problems in the lagoons around here. So get to it, and I'll see you in two hours. I'm headed to the little row of shops here in the resort. They've got just about everything. I'm glad you had a great day," Mavis said and walked away.

"Oh my gosh. I just about wet my pants," Natalie said.

"That's gross," R.O. replied.

"As if nothing you ever say is," Heather said.

"Let's go. I want to get this safe secured," Chris said not seeing the hotel clerk walk up behind him.

"Did you say you needed to use the hotel safe, sir?" the man asked.

"Yes, maybe I'll come over later," Chris responded nervously as the man walked away.

"Let's go," Natalie said in a firm tone.

Fifteen minutes later, they had located bungalow 14, with the two huts next to it, and had unloaded the luggage carrier. They stashed the safe, still cloaked in the ripped dive bag in one of the closets. Just as they were finishing, R.O. noticed through a window that Jack was walking on the beach. He took off after him.

"Cross your fingers," Natalie said as she watched him run to Jack, give him a big hug, and start talking.

"He knows better. He'll be quiet for now," Chris

responded hopefully. "Better go get some rest and clean up."

"Look whose talking, big boy," she said and gave him a peck of a kiss. "I'm starved so this Billy Fly's better be good food and lots of it," she said as she closed the door behind her and walked to her hut.

Chris walked over to the closet and slid the dive bag off the safe. He used his diving knife to cut the ropes that made the netting they had used to lift it. Once the ropes were off, he sat down on the floor and looked at the locking wheel on the outside. It resembled any other ordinary combination lock, but it had a handle that he thought must control the airtight mechanism for the safe. He carefully grabbed the handle, not wanting to break it off in case it had corroded. It didn't budge, and he couldn't see any corrosion on it. He raised his eyebrows in surprise. He carefully tried to turn the combination wheel, but it didn't move.

"We could always blow it open," R.O. suggested, walking back into the room.

"You scared me, little brother," Chris replied. "It's hardly even rusted or corroded. Amazing, and no, we can't blow it open."

"How about a welder's torch?" R.O. asked.

"Well that's a thought. But we'd have to get a welder to help. I've never used one, and I sure wouldn't want to get the metal so hot that if there were important papers about World War II inside, they would vaporize from the heat," Chris said.

"I hadn't thought of that," R.O. said. "Good thinking."

"Well, we've got two weeks to figure it out before we fly out of here. I don't think they'll let us check this on an airplane, and if we send it air cargo, customs has to look inside," Chris stated.

"We've got two weeks to get it open; then we'll be rich," R.O. added.

"I doubt it. It probably contains papers about troop movements or naval battle plans and stuff about World War II. It would be neat stuff for a museum to have to maybe shed some new light on the war in the Pacific," Chris said.

"That's boring. We need to find more treasure. Can't have enough of that," R.O. commented. He shed his clothes and headed to the shower in the bathroom.

Chris covered the safe and lay down on the bed. He instantly fell asleep.

Fifteen minutes later, he felt a tug on his T-shirt. He opened his eyes to a wet-headed R.O.

"Your turn. Better make it quick, it was running low on hot water," R.O. said.

"Gee, thanks." Chris checked his watch and noticed the amount of time R.O. had stayed in the shower. "Payback will be tomorrow," he said.

At a quarter till six, Heather and R.O. were leading the way to the restaurant with Natalie and Chris walking far enough behind to talk.

"What are we going to do with the safe?" asked Natalie.

"I don't know yet. But if those people in the other amphibian aircraft went back down to the ship, they'll notice the fallen wall right away. I mean if R.O. hadn't been chasing those fish and poking around, we would have never found it," Chris responded.

"You didn't tell him that did you?" Natalie asked.

"Are you kidding? He's insufferable enough about treasure as it is," Chris replied.

"You smell good," Natalie said.

Chris blushed, as usual, and smiled.

"Thanks," he said. "We both smell like the ocean though."

"I was hoping you wouldn't notice, Mr. MacGregor. It's a far better smell than the back of the fish truck in Hong Kong, wouldn't you agree?" Natalie replied.

"No doubt about that," Chris said as they entered the front of the open-air restaurant on the beach.

"Oh, Chris, do you remember our first dinner?"

"Well, it's only been six months; I think I can remember longer than that. D.J.'s on Grand Cayman," he replied as Mavis walked up.

"A sharp couple if I ever saw one," Mavis said in her British accent. "Follow me, Ryan and Heather just sat down, and your father is over here."

"Mom, I forgot to tell you how nice you look," Chris said.

She turned and looked at him.

"Thanks, sweetie," she said.

"How's your hand?" he asked.

"I told you yesterday, and the day before that, and the day before that, that it is all healed. I just need to get some strength back into it with the exercises the physical therapist showed me, and I'll be like new. Now don't ask me again. I have a mum; she lives on Harrington Court in London," Mavis said and then kissed him on the cheek.

"You smell good," she said.

Chris blushed again.

"Sorry, I didn't mean to embarrass our great outdoor adventurer," Mavis said, turning toward the table.

Soon everyone was seated and busy eating an appetizer of fried calamari rings that Jack had ordered for everyone. The waiter came and took their drink orders, who was then followed by an older gentleman with a dark tan and nicely groomed snow-white hair flowing down to this shoulders. He was wearing a silk shirt with a tropical print, white shorts, and black flip-flops. R.O. stared at the man's skin to see if his tan was painted on; it was real.

"I'm Billy Fly and welcome to my restaurant," the man said.

Jack started to stand.

"No, don't get up. I just wanted to come and meet the renowned Dr. MacGregor and his very large family, and such a beautiful wife," he said and took Mavis's hand and kissed it.

"Now Chris, this is a true gentleman," Mavis said.

"Have a good meal; I'll stop back by in a bit to see how things are going. The appetizer and your dessert tonight are on the house," Billy Fly said and walked away.

"What a nice man," commented Mavis.

"Yes, and I hear from my friends that he owns about everything around here," Jack said.

"I'm impressed," Natalie stated, still looking over the menu. "There is so much food and so little time to eat it."

"My thoughts exactly," Heather replied. "But at least I'm warm enough to eat it. I never want to go back to Alaska or China in the winter. I get chills just thinking about it."

"Hey Heather, don't you want to order a turkey sandwich like the one you ate at the Great Wall of China?" R.O. popped off.

"Oh, yuck. That pathetic, cheeseless turkey sandwich was horrible," Heather replied.

"Look Chris, there's that old lady with the cat," R.O. pointed out.

"Be polite, Ryan. We do not call elderly people old ladies and old men," Mavis corrected him, never looking up from the menu.

"Mom, you should have seen her use her spear gun. She was fast and accurate. She then cut the head off the fish and fed it to her cat right on the beach," R.O. explained.

"Ryan I am not even going to threaten you any more about lying and exaggerating. Telling you that I will send you to Georgia to your Aunt Marcia's will just fall on deaf ears. I don't know that I'll even assign you more homework while we're here since you're well ahead of schedule for the year. But I think I will start fining you like professional athletes get fined. I think for a little lie, I'll charge you five dollars. For an exaggeration, I think ten dollars will work. And, for the really big whopper, I'll take fifty dollars out of your travel money. How's that?"

R.O. didn't say a word.

Natalie thought that if Mavis knew about the safe, they all would be broke.

"Mom, she really did do all of those things," Heather said softly.

Mavis looked up from the menu. "She did?"

"That's right, Mom, she did," Chris answered.

"Uh, well, egg on my face . . . but the fines are still the new rule. Forgive me for assuming that you were exaggerating again, Ryan." Mavis winked at him when he looked up.

He smiled and said, "I think I want one of everything to eat."

"No, that's my order," Natalie said, and they all laughed.

Soon their appetizers were on the table. As they ate, they discussed the flight from China, Chris's three weeks in Australia, the many different wreck sites they wanted to dive, and Natalie's long telephone conversation with her mother the day before.

But not far away, in the depths of the sea, were forces that would soon affect everything in the lives of the MacGregors and Natalie Crosswhite, forces that would change them forever!

4

Billy Fly's

The second round of appetizer platters, consisting of mango, passion fruit, sliced bananas, nuts, and pineapple all covered with a sweet coconut milk sauce, disappeared quickly with the MacGregor crowd. R.O. started looking around for the main course when the co-owner of the establishment walked back to their table.

"Well, how's the appetizer? Everybody getting too full for the main event?" Billy Fly asked as he pulled up a chair from an adjoining table.

"It was delicious. I don't believe I've ever tasted a sauce for fruit that was as delectable as yours," Mavis commented.

"Thank you," responded Billy.

"May I ask for the recipe?"

"Sorry, that's a trade secret. It took me twenty years and that many cooks to come up with it, and I can't let it go now. One of my partners bottles and sells it in Honolulu," Billy said.

"Partners, do you have more than one?" Jack asked trying not to sound nosey.

"Sure. I've got Bill over there, who we call Young Deer,

his Cherokee name," Billy said, pointing to a tall handsome American Indian behind the drink bar.

"He's cute," Heather whispered to Natalie.

"And then I have a silent partner in Hawaii who shares the ownership of the hotel with us. Gary Bridwell and his son Cody own several hotels and a security company in Hawaii. Gary was my wingman during the war."

"Wow, that must be really neat. I would love to live in Hawaii," Heather said.

"Yes, it's nice, but I prefer the equatorial tropics myself. Life in Hawaii can be as fast as L.A.," Billy said.

"Or Dallas," R.O. joined in.

"You folks from Texas?" Billy asked.

"Yes we are. This is my wife Mavis, my two sons, Chris and Ryan, my daughter Heather, and our friend Natalie," Jack replied, finishing the introductions.

"But I detected a British accent from Mavis a moment ago. There's no twang in it, and you don't draw out your vowels, so you aren't Australian. You don't chop off the end of your words, so I guess you aren't South African either. So, it's got to be London. Crisp, clean British," Billy said.

"Very good Mr. Fly," Mavis said and smiled. "And from where do you hale?"

"Arizona," replied Billy.

"From the sand to the sea," Chris said.

"You just don't know how right you are," Billy stated. "I used to hate water but spending three years in the South Pacific during the war changed my attitude. Now I love it."

Staring at his arm, R.O. asked, "What does that tattoo mean?"

"Ryan, be polite," Jack said.

"That's alright. Kids are curious and ask. It's my old flying unit, the 339th during World War II. I flew a P-38 Lightning in the Battle of New Britain when we surrounded the Japanese at their big base at Rabaul not far from here. I was stationed for part of my war days in the Solomons and Port Moresby. When the war was over, I went back to Tucson and got a job. One day the temperature hit 110 degrees; it was so hot I was miserable. I thought about my days in the tropics, and even though we have warm days, we are never dry and the ocean is always right here. So I came back to New Britain and stayed," Billy said.

"What a great story," Mavis said. "Now you have a wonderful restaurant and hotel where once there was war."

"Exactly. It's never been easy, but I've had a good wife to help me and friends I've met who like this business, so I couldn't feel more pleased about it. Anybody hungry yet for the main course?"

"I am," Heather and Natalie said in unison.

"Me too," Ryan added.

"Then grab a plate and follow me over to the mumu pit," Billy said.

"What kind of pit? Did you say moo like a cow says moo?" R.O. asked as Mavis grimaced.

"No it's mumu. It's a pit that is usually dug on the beach or in the ground, and the wood is burned until it's charcoal. Then rocks are laid in with banana leaves on top of them, and we put in the food. It is usually pig, taro root, sweet yams, and a bunch of other veggies. Then we pour coconut milk on top of it. Since we aren't out on the beach, I have my own mumu pit right here in the restaurant." Billy stood up and started walking toward it.

Everyone grabbed a plate off the table and followed him. They caught up just as he reached the stone fence around the pit.

"Wow," R.O. said as he leaned over, feeling the heat coming off the hot stones in the pit.

"This is amazing," Natalie said and looked at Chris.

"I agree," Chris said.

Two native island waiters began unwrapping the food, and with three-foot-long spoons, forks, and tongs, they began serving the cooked food. As each person's plate was

filled, they walked back to the table where baskets of fresh-
ly baked rolls were waiting for them with pitchers of ice
water and lemons. There was little talking as everyone tasted the food that had been cooked over beds of rice.

"This is so good!" Natalie was the first to say.

"I agree," Heather followed with a full mouth.

"My, what a wonderful cacophony of tastes," Mavis said.

"Coconuts of taste?" R.O. asked.

"No, cacophony," Mavis replied.

"Means lots of them, right?" R.O. asked.

"Very good," Mavis said and took another bite.

"This pork is so tender and moist," commented Jack.
"What do you think, Chris?"

"I'm eating. I'll talk later," Chris said.

Fairly soon, the kids were headed back to the pit for a
second round, while Mavis ordered a cup of hot coffee.

"Well, what do you think?" Jack asked Mavis since they
were alone for a minute.

"This is truly a paradise, the warm breezes, the blue
ocean, the wonderful food. Truly unbelievable," she replied.

"I agree, but there's something that worries me. I talked to
Randy today, and he has isolated cyanide in the lagoons of
one of the islands nearby. It's beginning to affect the pearl
beds; he's concerned about the long-term effect on the
employees of the pearl company and nearby reefs. They
spend a lot of time in the ocean, and the exposure could be
deadly. It could also wipe out the sea life nearby."

"That's not good," Mavis responded. The waiter brought
her cup of coffee and set a full carafe in front of her.
"What's it from?"

Before Jack could answer, she said, "This gentleman
knows my weakness, lots of good coffee. I'm interested in
trying their house blend."

"It's my favorite," said a voice behind her.

Mavis turned to be greeted by an attractive older woman
wearing a silk floor-length gown.

"I'm Mrs. Fly and don't let me interrupt your dinner," she said.

"Oh no, we're just having coffee and maybe one of those beautiful pastries I saw when I walked in," Mavis responded.

"May I join you?" Mrs. Fly asked.

"Please," Jack replied. He pulled another rattan chair up to the table just as the kids were returning from the mumu pit.

"I'm Mavis and this is my husband Jack," Mavis said.

"Yes, Billy told me. Randy Heath is a good friend, and he said he was consulting outside experts on the pollution problem he discovered and so we kind of put two and two together. And please, call me Adi," she said.

"And this rogue crew is our children and one of their friends," Mavis said.

"That's Ryan, this is Chris, Heather, and here comes Natalie," Jack pointed out.

"You should see how much food Natalie piled on, Dad," stated Ryan.

"Be polite, Ryan," Mavis said quickly.

"What a wonderful family you have," Adi said.

"Yes, we are very proud of them," Jack replied.

"We were diving on a Japanese wreck today," R.O. said.

"You were, how fun," Adi answered.

"Yea, we saw so many big fish, and Chris flew through a rain storm to land in the lagoon," R.O. added and pushed a spoonful of rice into his already full mouth.

"Your son is a diver and a pilot? How wonderful," Adi said.

"Yes. He is quite accomplished," Mavis responded.

"Chris flew a helicopter across China," R.O. said.

"I am impressed," Adi said.

"What's that tattoo mean?" R.O. asked since he was sitting across from Adi.

"Ryan, I warned you about manners once. Don't push it," Jack responded quickly.

"Oh, that's O.K. It's my serial number from the World War II concentration camp where my family and I were held. It was Majdanek near the Polish town of Lublin," Adi answered with a somber look on her face.

"My dear, you are so brave," Mavis said quickly. "My parents remember the Blitz in London quite well but nothing like you have endured, I'm sure."

"Only my sister and I survived; then we went to Israel with friends to grow up. I met Billy at a World War II commemorative event when his air wing from the Pacific Theater joined air wings from Europe for a week in Israel. It was love at first sight," Adi said.

"How sweet," Mavis replied and reached out to touch her hand.

"Who knew that a little girl from Warsaw, Poland, would grow up in Israel and then move to the South Pacific?" Adi said as Billy walked up.

"I see my little wife discovered the MacGregors," Billy said.

"Yes, she did," replied Jack.

"We were just hearing about your romantic first meeting when you walked up," Mavis said.

"If he weren't so tanned, you could see him blush right about now," Adi replied.

"She always says that. A P-38 fighter pilot never blushes, and we don't flinch," Billy said and laughed.

"Well, we'll leave you to finish your meal. We like to meet everyone who comes to our restaurant," Adi stated.

"That's why we're so popular here in Gloucester and have repeat customers who are tourists from year to year. Especially all of the scuba diving enthusiasts," Billy added.

"It was great meeting you," Jack said as they walked away.

"What a charming couple," said Mavis. "You think we'll age that gracefully, honey?"

"I am sure we will," Jack answered and leaned forward for a kiss on the lips.

"I will lose my food for sure," Ryan complained as he watched his parents. "It's bad enough to see Chris and Natalie do it."

"Hey, watch out, buddy," Natalie said.

"Well, I'm headed for that beautiful pastry table over there," Mavis said and got up.

"Concentration camps, that's pretty heavy stuff," Chris said. "You guys remember the units that we studied on Nazi Germany and the Holocaust?"

"I do. It was horrible. I can almost see it right now," Heather replied.

"I remember reading the *Diary of Anne Frank*. It made me sad. But I liked the stories about how the American and British armies chased the Nazis across Europe. That was true courage," R.O. said.

"Ryan, I'm proud that you learned that from your lessons. We need examples of courage these days," Jack said.

"Chris is my hero," Natalie gushed.

"He sure is," Jack agreed. "This family will never be the same after what Chris did in China. I would have to say he qualifies as a superhero!"

"He is for sure, Dad," Heather joined in.

"What's everyone so solemn about?" Mavis asked as she returned with a dessert in her hands.

"Oh nothing, honey," Jack said. "We were just thinking about how great everything is."

"Well good. Then, let's see some smiles on everyone's face," Mavis said.

"Mom, that looks great. I'm headed to the pastry table," R.O. said.

"How can you eat another bite?" asked Natalie, leaning back in her chair.

"Well, because I didn't eat the whole pig," R.O. retorted and looked back at her.

"Just about the time I start to like him, the brat in him shows up," Natalie said.

"You don't have to live with him all the time," Heather added.

"Maybe I should reinstitute the homework for misdeeds

rule again. What do you think Chris?" Mavis asked and took a bite of the lemon pastry.

"I think it would be good for Ryan and Heather," Chris answered and smiled.

"Chris!" Heather exclaimed.

"I'm just kidding. We do need some way of keeping a leash on R.O. sometimes. The trip to Aunt Marcia's won't work anymore because no one has been sent there," Chris said. "And besides, she's moving to Arkansas."

"You're right. I didn't follow through so I think we need to go back to having more homework," Mavis replied. "Parents should follow through with discipline or it becomes a joke. Since I'm not a court jester of Her Majesty the Queen, but a loyal subject instead, I hereby declare that homework is back!"

"But I thought you just said we were caught up on the homeschooling bit," Heather said in a pleading voice.

"You have, but wouldn't it be nice to get even more ahead. Yes. That's what I'll do," Mavis said and took a sip of hot coffee. "Tomorrow we'll look at the courses we need to complete before we finish in London in six months, and we'll start them right away and just stretch them out more. Your father has work to do in Australia, New Zealand, possibly Mexico, and Scotland before we go back home to Texas."

"Whatever," Heather responded softly as she drank some water with lemon.

"What's on the agenda tomorrow?" asked Chris.

"I'm going with Randy Heath out to the pearl beds. Would you like to come?" Jack asked.

"Sure," Chris replied.

"Heather and I are going to lie out on the beach," Natalie said.

"Well, I guess it's me and Mr. R.O.," Mavis said and smiled. "He could stand a behavior tune-up. It's been a few weeks."

"Who needs a tune-up?" R.O. asked as he walked up.

"Guess who?" Natalie said, enjoying the little pay back from the whole pig comment.

"Time for Chris and me to hit the sack. We've got to fly out at five in the morning so we have a long day ahead of us," Jack said.

"I'll be in bed soon, Dad," Chris said as Jack and Mavis got up and walked away.

"How about a walk on the beach back to the bungalows?" Natalie suggested.

"I'm out of here," R.O. said and caught up with his parents.

"Well, y'all have fun. I ate too much, and the dive today wore me out. Natalie, don't come get me before noon because that's when I'm programming my eyelids to open. Good night," Heather said and walked away.

As Natalie and Chris left Billy Fly's and their feet sunk down in the fine sand of New Britain Island, they talked about their first night together, walking on Seven Mile Beach, Grand Cayman Island. Both nights, then and now, were after a great meal at a fine restaurant; they also remembered the night dive and the adventure that followed.

"I hope that never happens again," Natalie said as she turned to face Chris.

"Me too," he said and kissed her lightly.

"That seems like a long time ago."

"About six months is all," Chris said. "It won't happen again."

"I don't know. I think extreme adventure is what all of you MacGregors feed on," Natalie replied. "You guys are definitely adrenaline junkies!"

"No we aren't. We're just normal folks from Texas."

"You are so full of it, Mr. MacGregor," Natalie said and hugged him before kissing him good night.

5

Seashell Heaven

The next morning, R.O. was walking on the beach about one hundred yards ahead of Mavis, collecting all the unusual seashells he could spy. In the distance, he could see an all-terrain vehicle coming toward him at a moderate speed on the beach. As it drew closer, he recognized Adi. Once she reached R.O., she came to a stop. Seeing the handfuls of shells that R.O. had collected, she made him an offer he couldn't refuse.

"If you'll hop in, I'll take you to a spot on the beach where you'll find the best shells on New Britain Island," Adi said.

"Sure, let me ask my mom," R.O. answered.

He hopped into the ATV, spilling some of his shells in the seat. Adi drove the ATV down the beach to Mavis.

"Mom, Mrs. Fly wants to take me to find the best shells on the island. Can I go?" R.O. shouted as they approached.

"Absolutely," Mavis responded with a smile.

"Morning, Mrs. MacGregor," Adi said.

"Good morning to you," Mavis replied.

"We'll be gone a couple of hours, and I'll bring him back directly to the cottages," Adi said.

"That would be great. Have fun," Mavis said and winked at R.O. who waved bye.

After they had been driving for a few minutes, R.O. felt compelled to talk.

"Is it always this calm in the morning?" R.O. asked.

"Yes, but this month is the first part of our monsoon season so anything could happen for the next three months," Adi replied.

"Oh, I see," R.O. said. "How far is the spot where the best shells can be found?"

"It's about two miles down the beach," Adi replied.

"What was it like?" R.O. asked.

"What was what like?" Adi asked back.

"What was it like in a concentration camp?"

"Oh my, that's a big question for a boy of your age," responded Adi. "What are you, twelve, thirteen?"

"I'm thirteen, just last month."

"Well, where do I start?"

"How about when you were my age."

"When I was twelve, we lived in a big city in Poland, Warsaw," Adi answered. "My father was a jeweler and was known as the man who could make or repair anything. We lived in a large ten-room apartment over his business. I had two brothers and one sister, and I was the youngest. Then one day the Nazis came."

"I've read about the Nazis, so don't worry about exposing me to that kind of material," R.O. said, trying to sound like an adult. "We read about Hitler and World War II in Europe."

"Did you read about the Holocaust?" Adi asked.

"Yes, and we went to the Holocaust Museum in Washington, D.C. when my Dad was visiting with Congress about some environmental problems," R.O. said.

"So you know about the murder of over six million Jews in the concentration camps and in the cities of Europe at the hands of the Germans?" Adi asked, not wanting to shock a young boy with her story.

"Yes, I do. I've even see their shoes."

"Their shoes?"

"Yes, in the Washington museum there is a room that we walked through that had shoes tossed about on the floor. There were thousands of them. Mom explained that people wore the shoes into the prison but never came out. It made me cry. So all that was left were their suitcases, some personal belongings, and their shoes," R.O. stated.

"I see. I haven't been to that museum, just the one in Israel, my former home. We have many things like that there too," Adi replied.

"Was it hard to sleep in a bed with six other people?" R.O. asked.

"No, because they were all my family, and it made me feel safe, at least for a while," Adi said. "And we used bunk beds."

"Tell me about Warsaw," R.O. said.

For the next hour after they arrived at the beach with hundreds of beautiful shells, Adi told R.O. about growing up in a rich, free Poland, and she explained how it all changed once the Germans invaded and the Nazis persecuted the Jews. She told him how her father was singled out to repair watches for the Nazis officers and was forced to extract diamonds and precious jewels from the belongings of murdered Jews to be sent back to Berlin. She described the day the Germans built the wall to keep all the Jews in Warsaw in one place and how they would methodically roam the streets to take families to the trains.

"I read that the Jews in the ghetto fought back," R.O. said.

"Yes, we did. But we eventually ran out of weapons, food, and fresh water. Our efforts became futile. That's when my family was taken to the trains and sent to Majdanek to be imprisoned," Adi said as a tear formed in her eyes.

"I'm sorry. I didn't mean to make you sad."

"That's alright. I always think about my parents and brothers when I tell this story. They died in the camps. Only my sister and I survived to move on to Israel some time later. She still lives there and has four children. That makes me happy."

"Then I'm happy, too," R.O. said.

"You must be a good boy, Ryan."

"Call me R.O. Sometimes I get in lots of trouble. But I can't help it. My sister causes most of it."

"I just can't imagine that," replied Adi. "Well, we better get back. You've got quite a collection of pretty shells now, and you picked them up in about twenty minutes. It would have taken all day in the other spot. The current comes directly into the beach and, at high tide, leaves lots of shells here every week. The tourists find them sometimes, and other times they just stack up. A fellow on the island brings his tractor down here to scoop them up and uses them as a mix for cement. Pretty ingenious if you ask me."

The two talked a bit longer as the ATV hummed along the beach toward the hotel. Soon they could see Mavis lying on a reclining beach chair reading a book, and they drove right up to her.

"Hey, Mom, you should see all the neat shells I got. There were tons," R.O. said.

"I'm impressed," Mavis said as she got up to help him pick up the bucket out of the back of the ATV.

A few drops of rain landed on the beach as a passing cloud drifted by.

"Well, I was warned the monsoons might come early this year. Hope it doesn't spoil your stay," Adi said to Mavis.

"Oh, I don't think anything could spoil our stay after our visit to China, Mrs. Fly," Mavis replied.

"By the way, our last name is Pfleiderer. Billy used to go by Billy Fly when some islanders couldn't quite get the Pfleiderer out correctly. By the time I met him and we got married, he was Billy Fly," Adi said.

"Pfleiderer, one of those beautiful Swiss names, like the famous Pfund School for Girls in Bern," Mavis said.

"Exactly," Adi replied. "Well, have a great day, and I'll hope to see you all for dinner again tonight. There are many good restaurants on the cape, but we think we have the most diverse menu. Take care."

"Thanks for the ride," R.O. shouted as she drove away.

"Did you have fun?" Mavis asked.

"Yep, I did. I found lots of great shells, and Adi and I talked about when she was a little girl in Poland," R.O. said.

"You did? How was that?"

"It was sad, but I learned a lot. It was better than reading about it because she was there. I remember when we all went to Washington, D.C. to see all the monuments, the International Spy Museum, and the Holocaust Museum. We talked about that some," R.O. said.

"How was that for you?" Mavis asked again out of motherly concern, always questioning what the children are exposed to.

"It was good. I now understand more about why the Nazis did what they did and how really sad we should feel and why we shouldn't let something like that happen again."

"I'm glad you understand it, then," Mavis said, looking into his eyes.

"I do. We've seen some bad people in the countries we've visited who tried to hurt us. But we've also met a lot of good people who want to help us. That's the best part, meeting all the good people," R.O. said. "And finding all of that treasure, too. You know when we were diving on the shipwreck yesterday . . . uh, well it can wait."

"I know. R.O. the treasure finder," Mavis winked. "You wouldn't be hungry would you?"

"Man, am I. How'd you know?"

"I just had a hunch. Let's go find some kippers and kidney pie," Mavis said pushing her British accent on him as she did from time to time.

"Mom. Don't even go there. It's donuts or scrambled eggs and bacon," R.O. replied, putting his right hand on his hip. "I would even settle for a bowl of cereal."

"You would," she replied. "Well let's go find it."

As they walked toward the bungalows, Natalie appeared on the walkway with a beach towel and a bag of beach necessities.

"Good morning," Mavis said.

"Good morning. What's up with you guys?" Natalie smiled.

"We're headed to the dining room to get something to eat," answered R.O.

"Not a bad idea," Natalie said.

"Is Heather up yet?" Mavis asked.

"Nope. She was sawing some pretty heavy logs a few minutes ago. I think she is still catching up from China," Natalie responded.

"Well, let's go to it then, I'm starved," Mavis said.

They walked on the pathway through the lush tropical foliage. As it began to rain heavily, they ran the last twenty feet to the dining room. Little did they know that this was the last dry morning they would experience for quite some time and their last day of leisure, as well.

6

Long Island Pearls

───────────────◀▶───────────────

Marine biologist Randy Heath was behind the controls of the silver Cessna 208 Caravan Amphibian, equipped with pontoons and a special cargo hold to carry supplies and equipment for the pearl beds on Long Island, two hundred miles west of Cape Gloucester, New Britain, and one hundred miles east of Madang on the island of Papua New Guinea. Painted in bold red letters on the side of the aircraft was the name of the company who employed his services, Long Island Pearl Company, Ltd. There was a string of white pearls painted from the nose of the craft down both sides to the tail with a black pearl on the very end. Randy, Jack, and Chris had left at daybreak from Cape Gloucester for the two-hour flight. Jack, an experienced traveler, was asleep in the back seat while Chris talked to Randy about his job with the pearl company.

"Yea, I love it. I tried some other jobs in the marine businesses in California and Florida, but I found the pace of the work down here to be what I like. The company has pearl beds all over the South Pacific, and several of us try to monitor the water quality to keep the clams healthy and producing. A few private operators we contract with sell their pearls to our company in exchange for our expertise. The big Japanese pearl companies have their own marine biologists on staff so they tend to keep to themselves. It's a competitive market out there," Randy said.

"I think that's pretty cool. I've thought about marine biology or oceanography since my family likes to dive everywhere we can. But I also like aviation since I got my pilot's license for fixed and rotary wing aircraft," Chris said. "But then every time we vacation in New Mexico or Colorado, I remember how much I love the mountains."

"So you can fly choppers?" Randy asked.

"Yes, sir. I learned in Italy last fall," Chris replied.

"That's pretty cool. There's our island," Randy said pointing ahead and beginning to descend.

Jack started to awaken almost on cue as the Cessna skimmed across the water toward the island, approaching a series of docks and buildings built out over the water two hundred yards from the shore. As the Caravan pulled up next to a dock, a large, husky native islander, with long hair to his shoulders wearing only shorts, waited to tie up the pontoons. Once the engine was dead, the three climbed out of the plane onto the docks.

"Hey, Doc," the man said to Randy.

"Hi, Roosevelt, how goes it, man?" Randy asked.

"Can't complain. I pulled those water samples you wanted. They're in the lab," Roosevelt said.

"Thanks. I'll get with you before we leave," Randy said and led Jack and Chris down the dock toward the four buildings built around the large dock area on giant pontoons.

"Roosevelt is my all-around technician. He does just about everything for me from setting up a pearl grid and harvesting to working in the lab and keeping the boats running. He's from the Western Highlands of New Guinea. His tribe is afraid of water so it took me a long time to convince him to stick around. Now he dives as well as anyone."

"Afraid of water, yet close to so much of it," Chris said. "That's surprising. Where did he get the name Roosevelt?"

"He told me that there was a missionary to his tribe by the name of Roosevelt Wells from Manhattan in New York City, and he liked him a lot. So he adopted the English name as many of the tribesmen do. Here we are," he said, and they followed him into the open-air lab.

After showing Chris and Jack the operation and what they did in the buildings, he laid a chart out on a large table.

"Look at the bar graph. For several months, our water quality was perfect for what we do here, keeping the clams alive. Then we noticed that part of the beds started dying. On this map of the beds around the island, you can see the area hit the hardest. Down along here," he pointed. "To about here just a hundred yards from where we're standing right now," Randy informed.

"Where's the main current?" Jack asked.

Pulling out a bigger map, Randy unrolled it and weighed it down on both ends with two-pound diving weights.

"The current flows northwest to southeast along the coast of Papua New Guinea to the Admiralty Islands," Randy said.

"Have you checked for any point sources for the pollution?" asked Jack.

"Yes, I have, but politics controls a lot of what goes on around here," Randy replied.

"Where doesn't it?" Chris added.

"Right. But there are different governing bodies for the Admiralties, New Britain, and this island we're standing on," Randy said.

"Well, almost standing on," Chris said.

"I see on your chemical analysis charts that lead and cyanide seem to be prevalent in all of your water samples," Jack continued.

"Yes, if you'll look at these charts, you can see where we

have had positive hits on several toxic chemicals," he said as he unrolled another map.

"It seems to jump around," Chris noted.

"Right you are. That means that it is intermittent, not a constant stream," Randy said.

"That rules out volcanic waste," Jack said.

"You think so?" asked Randy.

"Yeah, I do. If you had an ocean floor vent open up with magma, then you would have a steady stream in one location for a certain period until the magma stopped and solidified. But if you had a point source polluter, meaning a factory or plant that could turn on and turn off the toxic waste, then it would fit your findings. My guess is that you've got an industry that's dumping, and they are doing it haphazardly, trying to cover their actions with the possible volcanic sources," Jack said.

"Are there any active volcanoes around here?" Chris questioned.

"Are there?" Randy responded and walked over to another bench to lean up against it. "This whole area is sitting on volcanic plates with sulfide vents."

"Sulfide vents?" Jack asked quickly.

"That's right. From the Indonesian end of New Guinea to the Papua end, there are dozens," Randy said.

Chris leaned over the maps.

Randy walked over to a work counter, retrieved a small card, and brought it back to the table. With a pen in one hand and the card in the other, he started marking small "Xs" on the map as he checked the coordinates on the card.

"Cyanide?" Jack asked.

"That's right. It was so small I didn't think about it," Randy said.

"If I'm not mistaken, this part of the world is home to the third largest gold reserves on the planet," Jack said.

"We are. But the gold mines in the Admiralty Islands won't affect the currents near our pearl beds. The gold mines on New Guinea are far enough away that we shouldn't see this high a concentration of cyanide," Randy said.

"But look at the marks. There's a current in the ocean that is carrying pollutants to Long Island, and it goes straight by Karkar Island, here," Jack said and circled the island on the map.

"Is there a gold mine on Karkar?" Chris asked.

"Not that I know of. Usually an operation that large is well known. It has to be licensed by the government, and the huge investment companies like to brag about them to lure more investors. I haven't heard a thing. There is a small oil refinery, however, on the island," Randy said. "There are also two active volcanoes and about fifty thousand people."

"I think we need to pay them a visit," Jack said. "Do you know any of the people there?"

"No, I don't, but it's only a one hour flight so why don't we go see them," Randy suggested.

"I'm up for it," Jack said. "That's why I'm here. You need help."

"Chris, why don't you help me put together some dive equipment in case I want to stop along the way and take some samples of marine life," Randy said.

"No problem," Chris replied and followed Randy into another room.

Thirty minutes later, the Cessna Caravan was skimming across the water and lifting into the sky. The three men talked about the problem, volcanic activity, and gold mining even though none of them was a geologist.

"When we get back to Cape Gloucester, I'll put a call into my buddy, Gary Houlette. He's a top-notch geologist, and he might be able to shed some light on the problem. I just saw him last month in China at the Three Rivers Dam project," Jack said. "Knowing a good geologist has come in handy from time to time."

"I remember Dr. Houlette from Egypt. Same guy?" Chris asked.

"Same one," Jack answered.

"You fellows must get around some," Randy commented as he began the descent to Karkar Island.

"Well, it's a special year for the family; they've been coming along on my adventures as I write my book," Jack said.

"Can you adopt me?" Randy asked and all three laughed.

The Cessna sat down adjacent to a building that appeared to cover ninety acres under one roof.

"That's a giant building," Chris noticed.

"Up to now, I never thought about it much," Randy said. "Now I wonder if they aren't trying to hide something."

He drove the plane up to the extended dock where three other amphibians were parked and pulled along side. Two men carrying automatic rifles walked down the dock and stopped next to the aircraft, not offering to tie them up. Chris got out, took a rope, and tied it to the pontoon and then moved forward and did it again. Jack stepped out next, followed by Randy.

"This is private property," one of the armed guards said loudly.

"Yes, I know. Tell your manager that Dr. Randy Heath wants to talk to him. I'm with the Long Island Pearl Company," Randy said.

The two guards looked at each other, and then one of them walked up the dock while the other remained staring at the uninvited guests. Ten minutes later, a man wearing a long white lab coat and a yellow hard hat appeared with the other guard and proceeded toward them. As he got closer, Jack could read the lettering on the hard hat, Karkar Exploration.

"I am the manager of this facility," the Japanese man announced.

"My name is Dr. Randy Heath from the Long Island Pearl Company and these are my colleagues," Randy spoke.

"You are a long way off from your pearl beds, Dr. Heath," the man replied politely.

"Yes, I am. We're having a small problem with some pollutants in the water, which are affecting our host clams.

We've even had a small fish kill from time to time. I'm wondering if there is something from this plant you're releasing in the water that may be harmful to my company's business," Randy informed.

"I assure you, Dr. Heath. There is nothing being released from this facility that is illegal or could harm your host animals," the man said. "Forgive me; I am Hiroshi Fujita, the chief scientist of this facility. If you would like to tour our plant, I would be happy to show you around."

"Yes, we would," Jack said quickly.

"Then please follow me," Fujita directed.

After they had walked the distance of the pier, they entered into a small room on the outside wall of the plant. Mr. Fujita handed each of them a hard hat and instructed them to wear it at all times.

"What type of facility is this?" Jack asked as they began to walk among a multitude of tanks, metal piping, and control banks full of instruments.

"We process a small amount of petroleum that is brought to us by ship from New Guinea," Fujita said.

"I see," Jack replied. "Where do you dispose of your waste products?"

"We are very efficient and have very little waste," was Mr. Fujita's reply.

Jack, somewhat familiar with oil refining from his recent trip to Alaska and his home state of Texas, kept a barrage of questions coming until they were about halfway through the building. Giant air vents overhead began to drown out their conversation, and Fujita handed each of them a package of earplugs and motioned for them to put them in, thus ending the questioning.

As they made a sharp turn to go back, Jack looked toward a thirty-foot high wall and then at Randy. He leaned over to Randy and signaled for him to take out an earplug, which he did.

"Feel the heat?" Jack asked.

Randy put the plug back in and nodded yes.

The chief scientist gestured for them to follow him, and soon they were back in the little room taking off the hard hats.

"See gentlemen, we have a very clean operation here," Mr. Fujita said.

"What's on the other side of the wall? And we only covered about half the facility on our walk," Jack said.

"That is proprietary information, sir. All facilities have company secrets. As to why we are so efficient, well, we wouldn't want our competitors to learn that, would we?" the man said diplomatically.

"No, I guess not," Jack replied but thought to himself, "Something here is not right."

"Then thank you for stopping by, and I do hope you find what is harming your pearl beds," the Japanese man said and smiled. "Our men will see you off and help you untie your aircraft. Have a good day."

Randy, Jack, and Chris walked out of the plant into the small rain shower that had drifted over the island. They were soaking wet by the time they got into the Cessna and were soon hopping across the waves to take off. Randy flew the aircraft at about three hundred feet as they circled around the old volcano on the island and headed east toward New Guinea. They were five miles off the island when Chris spoke quickly.

"Down there. Look. It's all silvery," Chris said.

"I see it too," Randy acknowledged and dropped down to one hundred feet.

"A fish kill. Hundreds of them," Jack said.

"But it's to the west of the island so whatever caused it can't be coming from the island. The currents are too far out here," Randy said.

"Did you feel the heat coming off that wall?" Jack asked.

"We all did, Dad," responded Chris.

"My first guess is that there is a geothermal vent on that island, and they might be using it to generate steam for their processing," Randy speculated.

"I noticed a salty film on the aircraft as we were getting in," Chris said.

"Now that you mention it, there was one," Jack agreed. "How'd I miss that?"

"You were thinking too hard about everything else we've seen today," Randy said. "I'm going to land, and we'll take a fish and water sample. If there's something toxic down there, we don't want to be diving in it."

"Right about that," Jack said.

Within fifteen minutes, Jack was standing on the pontoon, retrieving some of the dead fish and taking water samples, which he handed to Chris. They were now anxious to get back to Randy's lab and analyze everything. The Cessna had more than enough fuel to make it back to Cape Gloucester with a stop at Long Island. Over the next three and half hours, all three discussed the visit to the mysterious plant, the heat exuding from the wall, the relatively few number of workers present, and the noisy ceiling vents. All agreed there were more questions from the trip than answers and were already planning a return visit by boat the next day.

"You know, I was thinking about the heat. If they have a geothermal vent on that island, they could easily be burning all of their waste and then dumping the ashes at sea on the return trip of the oil tankers that drop off their crude," Jack suggested.

"That makes sense, but doesn't account for some of the chemicals we're finding that would burn off at high temperatures," Randy replied. "We'll just have to go back."

Meanwhile back on Karkar Island, Mr. Fujita entered a luxury office inside the plant.

"Did they leave?" a man behind a desk asked as Fujita walked in.

"Yes, sir. They are gone. Just some nosey biologists

complaining about dead fish and clams. I gave them enough information that they will continue up the coast into Indonesia, never finding the source," Mr. Fujita said.

"Very good. If they come back, kill them. Then sink the plane in deep water. Our operations on New Guinea are too prosperous, and we can't have anyone nosing around. Is that clear?"

"Yes, sir," Mr. Fujita said and started to leave the room.

"By the way, if you gave them too much information or showed them too much, I would advise you to call your family in Tokyo and bid them farewell. You'll be shark bait before daybreak," the man threatened.

"I understand, sir. Not to worry. We won't see them again," Mr. Fujita replied.

Akira Yoshida picked up the telephone and dialed.

"Hello, tell Nickerson that as soon as it happens, I want to know immediately. I'll be over to the mine soon. Don't forget to light the heliport for a night landing. We'll notify you when we are close. It's too risky to fly in by day anymore," Yoshida said and hung up the phone. "Nosey scientists. They could become a pain," he said to himself. "Or maybe not. But there are always remedies for curious pests."

7

Desert Sailor

When Jack and Chris returned to catch up with the family at dinner that night, Jack was exhilarated about the day flying over the Admiralty Islands. It wasn't long before Billy Fly, the proprietor of the beautiful resort and restaurant, joined them at their table and listened to Jack and Chris talk about their visit to the mysterious refinery on Karkar Island and the problems that marine biologist Randy Heath was having at the Long Island pearl beds.

"I've got an idea. Let me take you up the straights between Karkar and New Guinea for a few days. I haven't been out to sea in weeks; my boat just sits in the marina and gathers barnacles," Billy said.

"That would be great, but is it big enough for all of us for that long of a trip? It's three hundred miles and that would be several days by boat," Jack said, not wanting to travel by sea for such a long trip.

"Oh no, don't worry, my boat is a Bertram 670. It has two Detroit Diesels with 1,800 horsepower each, goes 36.5 knots, and holds 2,800 gallons of fuel. That gives us a full seventy hours at maximum speed and room enough for eight people with 1,200 pounds of gear," Billy said without taking in a breath.

"Wow," was Chris's comment.

"Double wow," Mavis joined in.

"Very impressive, Mr. Fly," Jack said.

"Hey, I said call me Billy. We can top off fuel at the Long Island Pearl Farm and still have enough diesel to roam up and down the coast of New Guinea for a week. Get your diving gear together and meet me at my marina at 5:00 A.M.," Billy said. "You can be my guests on the *Desert Sailor*."

"Five o'clock," Heather said loudly and then put her hand over her mouth.

"You'll get some sleep on board, so don't worry about it, sweets," Mavis said and smiled. "And remember, it's warm where we're going."

"O.K. then, five it is," Heather said and forced a smile, trying to save face for the outburst.

"Good. I'll tell my cooks to stock it with food and fresh water. She holds 350 gallons. I'll also throw in an air compressor for refilling our diving tanks," Billy rejoiced, visually showing his giddiness about the trip.

"You like to dive, Mr., I mean Billy?" R.O. asked.

"I sure do. Been diving for forty years out here," Billy replied.

"With my permission, as time wears him down a bit," Adi said as she walked up. "Sounds like a big trip. Billy is the best guide around since he and his buddy crash-landed on an atoll during World War II."

"You've had an exciting life, Billy," Mavis said.

"I sure have, and tomorrow is just another chapter as I see it. So y'all enjoy your dinner. I'll have the front desk wake you about 4:30. Good night," he said and walked away to speak to a nearby waiter.

"O.K., crew, finish your dinner and off to bed. Pack your gear before you hit the sack and bring only diving gear, two changes of shorts, shirts, etc. You know the drill. Chris, pack your survival gear, as will your father, and don't forget the new audio-equipped masks that I bought in Hong Kong," Mavis directed.

"We've already used them, Mom," R.O. said.

"How was it?" she asked quickly.

"Super," replied Chris. "I loved being able to tell R.O. to stop what he was doing and pay attention. The full mask with the digital receivers was fantastic. No leakage, the sound reception was good, no gargling or interference. You picked out a great set, Mom."

"I'll have to pat myself on the back for that one," Mavis said.

"Well worth the investment," Jack said. "The kids are much safer being able to talk to each other while diving."

"When you're finished eating, don't waste time hanging around. Get a good night's sleep. If you go soon, you'll get more than eight hours," Jack said.

"Just a fraction of what I really need," Heather added, dabbing her mouth with the linen napkin.

"If it's beauty sleep you're talking about, I agree," R.O. said and got up.

Heather gave him a fake smile and looked away. Soon everyone was in their respective bungalows digging through the suitcases and trunks that had made their way from the Caribbean, East Africa, Egypt, Alaska, and China to the South Pacific. Shortly afterward, the MacGregors and Natalie were sound asleep.

The telephones in the three bungalows rang softly early the next morning, as they were programmed, so not to be annoying. After all, a South Pacific vacation was to be devoid of the common annoyances of regular life. For the MacGregors, a ring or a beep could be from the telephone, a dive computer, a pocket tracking device, or a host of other mechanical or electronic sources.

But Heather still moaned to Natalie, "What are we doing?"

Thirty minutes later, the resort's minibus deposited them at the dock next to the *Desert Sailor,* the impressive Bertram yacht owned by Billy Fly.

"Good morning," he said exuberantly.

"Jolly good day to you, Billy," Mavis said as she directed foot traffic toward the sleek ocean-going boat.

R.O. stopped and looked up to the tower, which was eighteen feet above sea level, and the electronic and satellite antennas that waved around in a circle, keeping time with the swaying of the boat from the early morn-ing tide retreating out to sea. One by one they handed or tossed equipment to two of Billy's employees and watched them open storage hatches all across the deck and carry some down into the expansive cabin. Heather was the first into the cabin area, but she immediately walked back out.

"Mom, you've got to see the inside of this boat. I mean it is so gorgeous; I could live here all the time, all day long," she said.

"Take me down," Mavis said as she handed her back-pack to Jack and stepped down the staircase. For just a moment, memories of the yacht in the South China Sea rushed into her mind, and a cold chill ran through her. But just as quickly, she began to focus on Heather, and the thoughts faded.

"Man, what a place," Natalie said as she stepped into the main cabin.

"Sleeps eight comfortably," Billy noted as he came in. "Choose your beds, and I'll take what's left."

"Very generous of you," Mavis said.

"Hey, I rarely have this much company, and when I do, it's a bunch of doctors or bankers here just to go fishing, not a family on an adventure. I mean, this is what it's all about," Billy said and flipped the switch on the coffee maker.

"Oh, you are my savior," Mavis rejoiced when she smelled the coffee. "And it looks like it perks really quickly."

"It's a special coffee maker I had my cook order for me. It's nearly instantaneous for the first cup," Billy replied. "At my age, I need all the stimulants I can to wake up and keep going."

"I'll pass. I plan on going back to sleep as soon as possible," Natalie said.

"Who's sleepy?" asked Jack as he entered the cabin.

"I believe everyone is," Mavis answered. "So we're headed off to divide up the quarters."

"Well, I'll be up top if you need anything. I'll set the satellite coordinates for Long Island, and the computer will do the rest," Billy said and left the room.

Chris, who had already climbed up to the bridge to examine the console of advanced electronic equipment, greeted him.

"Pretty cool," he said as Billy reached the control deck and began punching the buttons on the console.

"Much more advanced than my old P-38," Billy said. "But that airplane could fly through a hail of shrapnel and take a beating without killing me."

"Why didn't you keep on flying?" Chris asked.

"Oh, I did for awhile. I owned several Cessnas, a Beechcraft Bonanza, and a Russian YAK 52, which I bought just for fun. It was built for stunt flying and was not a bad airplane. Adi asked me to sell it when we got married, and I did, but I told her I wouldn't give up diving," Billy said as the Bertram diesels fired up.

As the boat moved away from the dock, everyone below was already tucked into a sumptuous bunk fast asleep. Only Jack, Chris, and Billy were occupied with either planning a dive or operating the boat.

At thirty knots, the Bertram reached the Long Island pearl beds in just about six hours. As the boat pulled in for refueling, Mavis, Heather, Natalie, and Ryan, having slept the entire way, woke up hungry. Jack noticed that Randy Heath's airplane was tied to the same dock.

"It's past eleven, and we haven't had breakfast," Mavis said as she awoke and tossed her auburn hair. She put on a canvas hat and began to wake the others stirring in their bunks.

"I'm awake, Mom. You don't have to touch me," R.O. announced and hopped down from his bed. "Where's Dad and Chris?"

"They're topside where they've probably been since we shipped out," Mavis replied.

"Bet they're going to be tired and grumpy," Natalie said and followed R.O. across the cabin and outside.

"What a glare. I need my sunglasses," Natalie said, squinting at the tropical sun.

"Hi, babe," Chris said and slid down the ladder from the bridge.

"Didn't you get any sleep?" Natalie asked.

"Nope. I've been topside with Billy. He's an interesting guy. I wouldn't have missed it," replied Chris.

"I'm going to get my sunglasses," Natalie said.

"Here, use mine till you do," Chris offered. He took off his glasses and gave them to her.

"Aw, relief," Natalie said. "You are so sweet."

"Don't start that," R.O. said. "Where's the food."

"I've got some sandwiches the cooks made and lots of frozen food to prepare for dinner. You'll find the sandwiches in the storage bins and cold soft drinks in the ones with ice. We usually use those to ice down the bait or the fish we catch," Billy said.

While Jack and Billy greeted Randy and topped off the fuel tanks, Mavis supervised the search for the sandwiches, chips, pickles, and soda pop.

"So where are you headed?" Randy asked Jack.

"We're going to Karkar Island first; then we're following the dead fish trail to the mainland," Jack replied.

"Remember to be careful diving in the water around any fish kills you might find. Could be toxic to you and the kids," Randy warned.

"Don't worry, I won't let anything happen to them," Billy said.

"We want to get close enough to get more samples. I brought along a portable water chemistry set to determine some basic information. It won't quantify the real heavy stuff in the water, but it can tell me if we are on a trail," Jack said.

"After what we found yesterday, I think it's a mainland point source," stated Randy. "The government in New Guinea has been cracking down on pollution from all sources of mining, drilling, and manufacturing since the Aussies have gotten into the picture. Whatever is killing my pearl oysters could just as easily kill the entire Great Barrier Reef, which drives the marine ecosystem on the east coast of Australia and attracts billions of dollars in tourism every year."

"I want to encourage ecotourism, but I care more about the reef," Jack said.

"Food anyone?" Mavis interrupted as she stepped on the dock.

"Yes. I'm hungry," answered Chris.

"Dr. Heath, how about joining us? Mr. Fly's cooks made some wonderful sandwiches," Mavis asked.

"You don't have to ask me twice when it comes to food," Randy said and adjusted his cap to block the sun.

"Looks like clouds on the horizon," Billy said as he gazed to the west.

"Reports state they are the first squalls of the new monsoon season so you all better be careful out there," Randy said. "I plan on flying back to New Britain before they get here."

"My big Bertram can handle just about anything, except a full-blown typhoon. Monsoons are just another form of a rainstorm," Billy declared and began to climb back into the boat to get something to eat.

After a short lunch break and a quick walk on the dock for everyone to get their land legs back, Billy fired up the Bertram, and they were once again back at sea. This trip would be shorter than the long haul from New Britain. Karkar Island was only 120 miles away, just four hours with the big Detroit Diesels. According to plans, they would reach the island, drop anchor, and stay the night. Tomorrow they would begin their hunt for the dead fish trail they hoped would lead them to the source of the pollution. But with pollution, there are always greedy men who are dangerous to anyone who exposes them.

8

Life Beneath the Sea

———————⬭———————

Chris turned on his flashlight to get a closer look at the magnificent coral that ran for two hundred feet before it turned to make the outer bank of the lagoon. He could see several species of healthy coral and none that were sick from a contamination of any sort. White anemones danced in the current, waving back and forth as if beckoning the clown fish that called it home. Suddenly an orange-and-white-striped clown fish scurried from beneath a coral head and plunged into the anemone, quickly reversing itself to view out across the reef. One could almost envision a smile on its face knowing that it was safe. A large *Tridacna,* a giant clam, lie quietly on the bottom with its purple-spotted foot sliding out of its valves. The microscopic dinoflagellate algae living in the protruded foot were busily producing food for its massive host.

"Take a look at the giant clam, kids," Jack said. "The dark spots on its foot help it make food by photosynthesis when there isn't much filtering through its gills."

"Looks like Heather's ugly tongue to me," R.O. cracked and gave her a look.

"Don't worry, Mom, I'm using controlled constraint," Heather said with a mature tone.

"Good for you, sweetie. See how easy it is," Mavis said looking away long enough for Heather to make a face and stick her tongue out for Ryan to see.

"That's gross," R.O. said quickly. "You're a clam for sure!"

Mavis turned but didn't catch Heather's retort.

"Ryan," she warned.

Schools of yellow butterfly fish darted here and there nearly colliding with the divers. R.O. spied a sea slug, called a nudibranch, that had red projections coming out of its back. He swam to it and watched the four-inch creature undulate in the open ocean, trying not to attract too much attention from a likely predator. It twisted and turned in its awkward swimming motion as its red-spiked gills flipped back and forth with each new move. Finally, R.O. reached out and touched it.

"Hands off or it's no more diving for you," Mavis said quickly from ten yards behind him. "I just love this new audio mask, don't you honey?"

"Sure, Mom, they're great," R.O. replied faking a smile as he turned toward her.

"Dad, these look pretty good," Chris said as he inspected a large brain coral with the polyps recessed in each geometrically divided hole to avoid the bright sunlight.

"I agree," Jack said from twenty yards away. "I don't even detect the presence of parrot fish eating at the coral."

"Nope, no little piles of calcium carbonate dust on the bottom near the reef," replied Chris.

"Good job, son. You might make a marine biologist yet," Jack said proudly.

They were about a hundred yards from the *Desert Sailor*, which was anchored one mile off of Karkar Island inside the protected lagoon. The water temperature was nearly eighty degrees and visibility was two hundred feet. The sun was high in the sky. Schools of Moorish Idols, also called giant angelfish in some parts of the world, swam around them, showing off their wonderful black and purple colors and unique shape.

"Wow, look at that barracuda," R.O. said a few feet behind Jack.

"Stay close to me, son," Jack said. "Barracuda have been known to school in this part of the world."

"Don't worry, Dad. I face-off big fish with teeth all the time," R.O. said, trying to sound grown up for his dad.

"Where are the girls?" asked Jack.

"They're right behind me about twenty feet," Chris responded.

"Don't bother with us. We'll call you if we need you," Mavis said, enjoying her newfound independence with the radio masks.

Natalie reached out and tried to touch a curious sergeant major fish, but it swam away quickly.

"These are old volcanic tubes from the island," Jack said, pointing to the fingerlike tubes that were about three feet in diameter and ran across the seabed from the island. "This is molten lava that ran into the sea. Must have been quite an eruption to reach this far out."

"Or it could have been a thermal vent," Chris added.

"You're probably right," Jack said. "Look over there. There are at least a dozen more and some are smaller than this one. Thermal vents must be the answer, but as I study them, they seem to be pretty old, maybe over a century since the last eruption that could produce enough lava to drive out this far."

"But they're not active now so that can't be the reason for the fish kills," Chris responded.

As Chris and his father studied the volcanic tubes, R.O. chased more fish, and Mavis, Heather, and Natalie cruised along the bottom of the lagoon looking at everything. They secretly hoped to find an old glass bottle or some remnant of history.

Chris took out his big Teflon-coated dive knife from his right leg scabbard and began to pry at the tubes.

"Solid rock," he said.

Suddenly a whooshing noise made them all look up. It was a school of spinner dolphins racing across the surface. Two stragglers dove down and swam by them at a terrific speed.

"Everyone be still. They won't collide with you if you're still. They will come as close as they can and then veer off," Jack directed quickly.

"How wonderful," Mavis said.

"Wow. I can't say wow enough," Natalie said as she turned and faced one coming right at her. "Oh my gosh."

"That was so cool," Heather said as another dolphin turned, swam around her, and then came to a stop next to her. She reached out and touched the dorsal fin, and the dolphin took off with two big kicks of its powerful caudal fin.

"Everybody surface for a minute," Jack said.

Each diver began to watch their smallest bubble and ascend from where they were. Since they were no deeper than thirty feet, decompression was not necessary, and they reached the surface quickly.

"Look toward the breakers," Jack said as he cleared the surface.

Everyone turned to watch the spinner dolphins ride the surf toward the beach; then at the last moment, they leapt from the grasp of the ocean and spun dramatically, some making three full turns before splashing hard into the water.

"Why do they do that, Dad?" asked Heather.

"Some scientists believe they do it to free themselves of external parasites; others say they do it for fun. Who knows!" Jack said and grinned.

"I think it looks fun," Heather added.

"Whatever the reason, it sure is fantastic," Chris stated. "Maybe a marine biology degree *is* in order for me."

"That would suit me just fine," Mavis said.

"Well, you know how I feel about that," Jack added.

"O.K. Everyone let the air out of your vests and descend to thirty feet. We'll regroup there and swim along the inside wall of the reef and circle back to the *Desert Sailor*. My dive computer says we have about thirty-five minutes of bottom time left and plenty of air."

"Roger, Dad," R.O. was the first to say.

"That's what mine reads too, Dad," Chris said.

Once on the bottom, everyone stayed close together as Jack and Chris peered into every nook and cranny of the reef. Circling around a coral head, they swam through a short grotto where the sun shown through the openings above allowing the sun to peak inside. The breathtaking vistas of the ocean world caused each one to chatter endlessly about what they saw knowing they were true aquanauts experiencing the ocean world firsthand and not through a glass-bottom boat or the porthole of a tourist sub.

An occasional spiny lobster would scoot quickly into a small cave while a curious moray eel would stick out its head and expand its gills, showing its sharp teeth. While extended, tube feathers, filtering whatever food they could from the water, would suddenly detract inside the tube, making the creature look like an inanimate object of little interest.

"Did you see that big one?" R.O. asked excitedly.

"Big what?" Heather answered quickly.

"A moray. Must have been ten feet long with a mouth big enough to swallow a football," R.O. replied.

"Watch the exaggeration," Mavis said quickly.

"No exaggeration, Mavis," Natalie added. "It was huge."

"Thanks, Natalie. You just saved Ryan from paying a fine or writing a paper about Polynesian culture before the arrival of England's glorious Captain Cook," Mavis said without taking a breath. "In fact, I didn't assign any homework the whole time we were in China. School is back in session. This is exciting."

"Mom, what a bummer. I still say that I thought you said we were caught up," Heather pleaded as a lionfish appeared from a coral crevasse and seemed to float in air, its featherlike fins extending in all directions.

"Watch that fish," Chris quickly warned. "It'll sting you, and you'll be sick for a month."

Jack turned to watch the small but beautiful fish with spines pointing out from its body.

"Chris is right. The lionfish is dangerous. Some call it a turkey-fish. No touching. Descend and swim under it if you need to," Jack warned.

"It is so beautiful," Mavis said as she passed five feet under, continually looking upward.

After twenty minutes of inspecting the lagoon, everyone had eight hundred pounds of air left, near the safety limit, and the veteran divers began to surface. Suddenly a ten-foot white-tipped reef shark appeared from the middle of the lagoon. Natalie was the first to see it.

"Shark alert," she said quickly. "White-tip at nine o'clock."

"Got it," Chris replied and quickly moved back toward the girls, placing himself between the marauder and the rest of them. Jack turned right behind him and was only three feet from him when the shark made its first pass over the group.

"Wow, that is so very cool," R.O. said and started to swim toward Chris.

"Stay put, Ryan," Jack barked quickly as Mavis, Heather, and Natalie all stationed themselves about four feet off the white sandy bottom of the lagoon between Chris, Jack, and the reef wall.

All the fishes of the reef began to scurry about zigzagging here and there in a defense pattern against the shark. Within a few seconds, all were safely hidden in the small caves of the reef.

The shark turned at the top of the reef, cruised back toward the divers, and then dove toward them quickly. Chris and Jack had their knives in hand as he made a quick pass straight at them. The distance was closing fast.

"Here he comes, Jack," Mavis said nervously in her mask microphone.

"Stay cool, Mom," Chris replied as the shark closed at a speed of twenty miles per hour.

Jack positioned himself shoulder to shoulder with Chris. The shark lifted its nose, pulled down its pectoral fins and opened its mouth, with both eyes covered by a membrane called nictatins, which closes only during an attack or a feeding frenzy.

"Ten feet, five feet, now!" Jack yelled.

At exactly the same moment, Jack and Chris kicked forward and up to gain the advantage over the medium-size shark. With its eyes closed, it instinctively lunged forward for an easy bite not knowing that its target had moved, but the two divers changed their position enough to avoid the jagged razor-edged teeth by inches and drove their knives hard into the nose of the shark.

Reacting from the sudden pain, the shark jerked right and then left with teeth still extended and with a lucky bite clamped down on Jack's left fin, just missing his foot. Chris was now astride the dorsal fin, his tropical weight wet suit tearing against the rough skin of the shark. With stab after stab, he was trying to distract the man-killer from its next target, his family floating unprotected against the reef.

"Oh my, gosh," Heather screamed into her mask.

Mavis reached out for her hand and missed, her eyes glued on the struggle ten feet away.

The spinning of the shark created a wall of bubbles with the two divers tightly enclosed. Jack pulled his foot back and his fin came off, with the short part where he had his foot falling to the sandy bottom. The shark was now more interested in its new passenger as Chris was slung about like a bull rider at a Texas rodeo. On the fourth twist, with a lucky stroke, he sank his knife deep into the side of the shark below the cartilaginous ribs and into the massive liver.

Blood began to pour out of the wound, and the shark turned one last time and fled for the center of the lagoon.

As it left the fight, one flick of the tail dislodged Chris's mask, and it was gone.

Chris felt around for the hose to the regulator when suddenly he felt someone hand him the mask. He pulled the straps back over his head and blew hard to purge the water from it. His eyes burned from the salt and he blinked several times before he saw Natalie a few inches away looking in.

"You all right, big boy," she said and smiled.

"I think. Let me count my fingers and toes," Chris replied, seeing blood pooling in the bottom of the mask.

"You've got a nice cut above your left eye," Natalie said as Mavis swam up.

"The shark's tail must have got him when it left," Jack added from behind Mavis.

"We need to get up and out quick before the blood in the water attracts more of his cousins," Heather said with a frightened tone in her voice.

"Good thinking, Heather," Jack said. "O.K. Let's go. Make a slow ascent."

"Dad, are you alright?" R.O. asked as he examined the chewed up fin he had retrieved from the bottom of the lagoon. "Hey, Chris, there's your knife."

"I'll get it," Mavis said and dove to the bottom a few feet below them.

As they were all ascending, she handed it to Chris and then patted him on the cheek. She then handed him her octopus spare regulator, knowing that he practically exhausted all of his air in the fight with the shark.

"Thanks, Mom," Chris said. He adjusted his new mask and took a deep breath after clearing the regulator with a quick blow.

"I think I know three different young men named Chris: Chris, the sweet son; Chris, the good student; and Chris, the fearless adventurer. I like them all a lot," Mavis said.

As they quickly swam on the surface the final fifty yards,

they boarded the boat while Jack kept a look out for more danger. All were welcomed by the smell of cooking sausage but still had quivering nerves from the shark encounter.

"Let me tend to the cut on your eye, honey," Mavis said as she gently lowered her tank onto the deck and stacked her vest and other gear on top of it.

"Oh, everyone, be careful with the new masks, and don't break the audio equipment," she said and looked at R.O. "They're over five hundred dollars each, and I don't want to replace a single one of them. I guess the shark didn't know that, did he?"

"I won't, Mom. Why do you always single me out?" R.O. asked. "No, don't answer that," he said as he carefully put his mask in its protective bag.

"Anyone for fried eggs, sausage, and biscuits, and what's this business about a shark?" Billy asked as he walked from the galley.

"Real food and not Mom's hotel granola breakfast," R.O. said.

"Chris and Dad fought off a monster shark, and I'm so starved," Heather said and followed him back to the main cabin.

As each added to their story about the white-tipped reef shark, they dove into breakfast. It only took the divers thirty minutes to devour the late breakfast as they excitedly shared what each had seen in the lagoon and how rare it was for a shark to attack divers. The energy from the bagels they had eaten before the dive had all been burned by the underwater swim across the lagoon and the surface swim back. It was now 2:00 in the afternoon, and the clouds became darker.

It wasn't much longer before Billy was back on the bridge piloting the boat. Mavis was in the kitchen cleaning up, with Natalie, R.O., and Heather asleep. Jack and Chris were plotting their course toward New Guinea in search of a dead fish trail. Only one hour into the two-hour slow and methodical trip across the strait adjacent to the vast lagoon, the first of the fish kills appeared.

"That didn't take long," Billy said. A light shower then began to fall. "Here, Chris, help me snap this wind and rain guard into place. Every time this happens, I wish I'd bought the enclosed bridge model. But nine months of the year, I never need it, and I figured it would be too hot without the wind in our faces. Adi says the wind will just make me look older."

"This will work fine," Jack replied as Chris snapped the last part of it in place.

"Keeps the charts dry, but they are mostly all laminated in plastic these days. Gone are the old paper charts, and I use the satellite ninety-nine percent of the time anyway," Billy said.

"Guess we'll be diving in the rain," Jack said. "Let's go."

"You boys be careful. I'm saving my energy for a dive when we get closer to New Guinea. No need to exhaust an old man too soon," Billy said and patted Jack on the back.

"I hope I am as full of energy as you when I reach your age," Jack replied.

Chris and Jack put on their gear while a warm tropical shower fell. Ten minutes later, they were in the water and leveling out at sixty feet under the boat. Jack checked his dive computer to be sure they hadn't exceeded bottom time for the day. The channel was about seventy-five feet deep and was on the outer edge of the Karkar Island lagoon. The water was still clear and warm, the ocean surge was minimal, and the current barely detectable.

"All's well along here. Lots of reef fish, coral appears healthy, and tubeworms have color and are active. There's a little bleaching in some of the coral, though. Could be a warm ocean affect rather than a toxin. I'll have to see if anyone is studying that. On the surface of things, I can't see anything wrong," Jack noted.

"I agree. The dead fish on the surface don't seem to be from this part of the lagoon," Chris agreed.

"O.K. Let's go back up and keep moving closer to the big island," Jack replied.

"Roger," Chris said.

Once on the *Desert Sailor*, Jack again looked over the chart, studying the direction of the southeasterly current. Chris went into the cabin to lie down for a quick nap. Natalie walked up and knelt next to his bunk.

"Getting tired yet?" she asked.

"Yes, after two dives, I'm beginning to feel the fatigue," Chris replied.

"That shark encounter really scared me, Chris MacGregor," Natalie said and reached out to rub his right forearm. "It made me think more about how I feel about you." She lightly brushed a finger across the bandaged cut over his eye.

"Why?" asked Chris.

"I've had other boyfriends before. I mean I dated all through high school, and then when I went to Oklahoma State, I met a couple of guys I liked a lot. But ever since we met last summer in the Caymans, I've never felt so in touch with someone before. Someone I could admire and respect. You're a special person, Chris," Natalie said and squeezed his hand.

Chris rolled over on his side and looked into her blue eyes.

"I've never been close to any girls. You're the first," he said.

"I hope there's never a second," Natalie said quickly.

Chris leaned forward and kissed her softly on the mouth.

"I'm pooped. Wake me in thirty minutes," he said as he leaned back.

"You've got it. Thirty it is," she said and left.

The boat cruised along smoothly with its two big diesel engines humming in the rear with Shark's Leader Two William Pfleiderer, World War II aviator and sailor at the helm. Jack began to see a pattern; the fish kills were appearing every four miles. Chris joined him after a short nap, and they stared at each other with puzzled looks after Jack explained the pattern.

"This is so strange. I mean every four or five miles we hit a patch of dead fish. It's almost as if someone is timing when they poison the fish," Chris said.

"I think you've got something," Jack replied. "Someone isn't continually dumping poison or there would be a longer string of fish each time. It's like a spigot or valve being turned on and off."

"A pipeline with a switch or small barges making timed dumps to avoid suspicion," Billy Fly said as he joined them.

"Shouldn't you be at the wheel?" Chris asked.

"I've got your little sister driving the *Sailor*. She's got a pretty good eye," Billy said and smiled.

"Heather?" Chris replied.

"Yup, she is now Captain Heather MacGregor," Billy said. "She'll be alright for a few minutes. I think we've got a pipeline of toxins that are being turned on and off to avoid suspicion."

"You may be right. We'll follow the fish trail until it stops; then we'll move toward the shore looking for the pipeline," Jack said.

"But where does the pipeline come from?" Chris asked.

"That's the million dollar question," Jack replied as the rain came down harder and the waves became choppy.

"Billy," Heather yelled from the bridge above the deck.

"Guess your sis is getting nervous about the weather change. Better go rescue the captain."

"We're getting close," Jack said. "I better call Randy and tell him. He may want to be in on this."

Jack walked into the cabin where it was dry and relatively quiet and picked up the satellite telephone. After a few seconds, a voice crackled on the other end.

"Long Island Pearls, Randy Heath speaking."

"Hey, Randy, this is Jack MacGregor," Jack replied.

"Hi, Jack. Did you find the source yet?" Randy asked.

"We're getting close. I thought you might want in on the finale," Jack said.

"Sure do," Randy replied. "What's your coordinates, and I'll fly out to meet you."

Jack looked down at the map and read off their longitude and latitude.

"When you get close, call us and we'll guide you in," Jack said.

"Roger that. It'll take me about three hours so I'll have to wait until in the morning. I wouldn't get there until just about dark, and if I hit a big rainstorm, it would be a little tricky finding you," Randy replied with an upbeat tone in his voice, hoping this was the end of the pollution problem.

"Tomorrow will be fine. We'll drop anchor and get some needed rest tonight. See you in the morning," Jack said as he hung up the radio telephone and turned to Mavis. "We've got a few hours before dark so break out a deck of cards and find out who's interested in a few rounds of poker."

"And just what do you intend to wager while you're teaching your children a very bad habit," Mavis said sternly.

"How about macaroni," Jack replied. "I saw a big bag in the cupboard and since there is no value then nothing is won or lost."

"Macaroni? Now this is a side of you that I've never seen before," Mavis responded and started to laugh.

"I'll play, Dad," R.O. said from behind him. "Chris showed me how to play poker once."

"Chris MacGregor! Well, O.K. But it's just for macaroni and nothing else," Mavis said.

"Count me in too," Billy Fly said as he walked up from behind. "I've never won any macaroni in a poker game before. Should be fun."

"Boys will be boys," Mavis said, walking to the cupboard to retrieve the big bag of macaroni.

Natalie walked up from the forward cabin where Chris had nodded off to sleep earlier.

"Did I hear something about macaroni and cheese for supper?" she asked.

9

Dirty Gold

The Sikorsky S-76C flew at tree-top level over the dense canopy of the New Guinea rainforest. In the grey light of dusk, the pilot kept a keen eye on the lookout for a flock of birds that might suddenly take flight and collide with the sleek blue and silver aircraft. The ride over the jungle was like a roller coaster as he maneuvered across the undulating terrain, a combination of mountains and extinct volcanoes that defined the landscape of this giant island, the second largest in the world. He kept glancing down at his radar double-checking the location and altitude of the peaks in his path.

"We should be there in about twenty minutes," Akira Yoshida said into the satellite telephone. "Have you found the main vein yet?"

"That's the surprise I had for you. Remember it was only two days ago that the ore suddenly changed from higher grade to producing nuggets. I haven't seen anything like it since the early days in the Canadian mines," Jon Nickerson said.

"What are we talking about; I mean what's the estimated

production?" Yoshida asked, not wanting to wait to hear it upon landing.

"You're familiar with Lihir Island aren't you?" Nickerson asked.

"Of course, don't bore me with questions," Yoshida snapped back.

"This mine will produce two hundred times the raw gold on Lihir Island's best day," Nickerson said calmly. "But it will also produce high-quality nuggets. No other mine in this region has done that."

"That is much higher than we expected when we built the geothermal plant to generate our own energy for the mine," Yoshida said.

"Exactly. With this higher grade, we can bypass the grinding circuit and pressure oxidation in the autoclaves, that is, if we decide to keep doing so. It is of such high quality that we can cut it from the volcanic rock with a pickax and hand-carry the nuggets out of the mine. The formation in the volcanic caldera is nearly perfect. It amounts to millions of dollars of gold per day, nothing like I've ever seen before," Nickerson said.

"I knew that hiring you would prove to be right," Yoshida said into the telephone. "I'll be there soon." He turned off the telephone and placed it inside his coat pocket.

As the sun began to dip below the horizon, the pilot of the Sikorsky began looking for the landing lights. A flock of blue parrots majestically flew across the helicopter's pathway a safe one hundred yards away. It was late in the day, and they were looking for a place to roost for the night. Searching the dense rainforest was tough for the pilot but even more so with limited light.

"I've got it," the pilot said into his headset so that Yoshida would relax. He knew the temperament of this man, who always carried hundreds of dollars of cash in his pocket and a .32 caliber Beretta Tomcat tucked securely in a holster on his belt. Toting a clip of hollow-point rounds with over nine hundred feet per second muzzle velocity, the little Tomcat could growl like a Kalahari lion!

The Sikorsky hovered over the small heliport, which was cut out of the overgrowth of the rainforest. The mine was virtually invisible from the air; all of the excavation was being done in the cavernous underground of a once active volcano. Setting the aircraft down carefully, the pilot immediately began to shut down the controls. The landing lights of the heliport went black. Yoshida opened the side door and stepped onto a hard metal surface that had been painted black to camouflage the landing pad with the volcanic terrain. By day, it would appear only to be a small opening in the forest.

As he stepped away, several men ran out to tie down the helicopter. Suddenly the heliport began to move, and the forest canopy opened, revealing a small hangar. The tracks of the heliport platform pulled the twenty-foot disc into the hangar. Once inside, a large camouflage net was draped across the opening. Yoshida smiled at his little invention and walked across the crushed black lava rock that had been pressed into the spongy floor of the rainforest to hide the entrance to the mine.

Seconds later, he entered the three-canopied rainforest to the jeering of a Yellow-billed Kingfisher high above him. He marveled at how quickly the jungle had grown back after they had moved all of the mining equipment and the hundreds of people who worked there into the caves below. Ahead of him, he could see two armed men holding open a door in the side of a rock outcropping at the base of the old volcano. Stepping through the door, he was immediately aware of the noise of machinery at work and the heat from the volcanic geothermal plant. The pleasant air of the rainforest had changed into a sulfurous stench of eighty-eight degrees Fahrenheit.

To his right was a descending corridor that led to the main cavern below. It was a long tunnel with two sets of metal doors but large enough to drive a truck through. He soon reached the guards' sleeping quarters and canteen. As he walked through, he was refreshed with the cool air-conditioning and stopped to drink a bottle of cold water. Moving farther into the mountain, he followed the main tunnel until it opened into a large cavern, and before him stood a menacing figure indeed. Jon Nickerson, a tall former professional Rugby player with the smile of a celebrity and a handshake of a mining engineer, greeted him. Dressed in a khaki shirt and pants with black boots laced to his knees, he sported a Beretta 9mm pistol in a shoulder holster under his left arm.

Looking at the weapon, Yoshida commented, "I see you come ready for any employee disagreements."

"You and I both know that this secret operation must remain unknown in order for us to maximize our profits. The Papuan government has no clue what we're doing. The Canadian bankers who backed this project don't either. Even the Australian mining company who gave us this equipment doesn't know! They think we're processing low-grade ore on the Admiralty Islands and paying half to the government. So the reality is that if one man or woman walks out of this cave before we are counting our gold on a ranch in Argentina, then we lose," Nickerson said and smiled.

"I agree. How prepared is the security force?" Yoshida asked.

"I have twenty-eight armed men stationed throughout the caverns. Three of those are near the vein we hit two days ago," Nickerson replied.

"Take me there," Yoshida said.

The two men walked through part of the five hundred-yard-long main cavern, with a ceiling of seventy-five feet. It was filled with walkways, equipment, tanks, and a barracks large enough to sleep and feed one hundred workers. As they entered another cave, the heat increased to ninety degrees.

"Are the ventilators working?" Yoshida asked loudly over the noise of the machinery.

"When the temperature reaches eighty degrees, they kick on," Nickerson replied. "But they're not exactly efficient. The temperature can spike to one hundred degrees pretty swiftly if the volcanic base surges through this side of the mountain. I mean, that's real molten magma just on the other side of that rock wall straight from the heart of the earth."

At exactly that moment, four large fans began to churn and a cooler breeze of eighty degrees began to flow through the cavern.

"That's much better," Yoshida said as he took off his coat and loosened his tie. His shirt was already soaking wet from sweat.

"That's about as cool as it gets. The geothermal generation plant is in the next cavern, and we have to rotate people out every three hours to avoid heat exhaustion. We pump water from the underground river that runs through there to convert into steam, giving us all the power we need," Nickerson explained.

The Japanese industrialist turned to the tall Canadian and stopped walking.

"You forget that this whole operation was my idea. There is no need to explain it to me," Yoshida said.

"Yes, but you rarely visit, and there have been some changes. I decided not to use a pipeline as previously planned." Nickerson replied. "Not only can we use the river for water to fuel our steam engines, but it serves as a nice reservoir to dump our waste."

"You fool," Yoshida shouted angrily. "That is why I was visited yesterday by scientists tracking cyanide poisoning in the ocean. You've left them a trail of breadcrumbs to find us."

"Don't worry. There are over a dozen gold mines in these mountains, and most of them are dumping into the rivers that lead to the ocean. By the time they trace it to us, we'll be millions richer and raising cattle in Argentina," Nickerson answered.

"I certainly hope you're right and that it will be you who

raises the cattle," Yoshida said and began walking again.

After the two men had walked two hundred yards through the caves, they came to the entrance of a small hallway into the mountain.

"Through here," directed Nickerson. He led the way past three armed guards sporting Colt M-16 automatic rifles.

The passageway traveled twenty feet before opening into a small cave that had a string of lights across its width. As Yoshida walked in, two men stopped working with their pickaxes and looked at him. They stepped back quietly. Yoshida walked up to the wall and touched it.

"I've never seen a vein like this before," he said.

"The sulfide vents of this old volcano are thick with gold ore but to actually find a solid vein is rare. It can happen, but it's very rare," Nickerson said as he bent down and picked up two gold nuggets the size of golf balls. "Pure gold. We assayed it, and it is right in there with Klondike gold. You're holding ten thousand dollars."

"How much have you already taken?" Yoshida asked quietly.

"Well let's say the bags already fill the back of a small pick-up," Nickerson smiled.

"It would take thirty years to harvest that much gold from low-grade ore," Yoshida replied. "What's your plan?"

"We chip away at this vein as long as we can. It could go black in one day, one hour, or it might last for a month. We already have enough to be wealthy forever, but I want to take out of here all we can. We have ceased the other mining operation completely so there will not be any more dumping in the aquifer. The aquifer must surface in the jungle somewhere and run into the ocean. We made our last dump two days ago. It should already be there by now," Nickerson said. "What about the workers?"

"We hold them until all work in here is done. When we destroy the mine, they go with it," Yoshida said, forgetting the two workers in the cave.

He quickly turned to them, pulled out the Beretta Tomcat

and fired off two quick rounds. The men fell dead to the floor of the cave.

"My mistake. Replace them, and dump these two in the river," Yoshida said calmly.

"No problem," was Nickerson response as he watched Yoshida holster his weapon. "Follow me. I've got air-conditioned quarters now. I estimate that we'll have about fifty million in gold within two more days. Staying beyond that time with this many people down here risks someone escaping to the top. Besides we've had some tremors from the volcano, and I wouldn't want to be down here if she decides to liven up a bit."

"Lead the way," Yoshida replied. "We've got some planning to do on how to get the gold out of the country. I can pay off Indonesia much easier than Papua New Guinea."

As they walked out of the massive cavern, the floors and walls began to rumble. Both men stopped and looked around as the trembling ceased.

"Not much time left," Nickerson noted. "I'll add five more men to the vein."

"I agree. Add ten. Time is what we don't have any longer," Yoshida said.

10

Dead Fish Ahoy!

The sun had been up only two hours when the rainstorm became a squall with winds reaching forty miles per hour, rocking the *Desert Sailor* back and forth. Billy Fly, Jack, and R.O. were dry and secure on the bridge, but Chris was high in the "crow's nest" of the Bertram in a rain parka and holding a pair of waterproof binoculars in his hands. Billy turned the boat and took the waves head on with the sturdy Bertram charging through every white-capped wave.

"Man, that was a big one," R.O. quipped as the bow of the boat ripped through a five foot swell.

"Oh, she'll take on waves bigger than that one," Billy replied.

Jack looked up at Chris who was riding high and keeping a sharp eye out for any dead fish trails. They were reaching the far edge of the lagoon where open ocean swells would be dangerously high when suddenly the wind slowed considerably, leaving only a light shower of rain. Mavis stuck her head out of the cabin below.

"What happened?" she asked.

"The storm passed over us. Now we're just in a slow

rain, typical of the beginning of monsoon season. Sorry, but I think your sunny vacation just ended," Billy answered.

"But it's still warm," hollered Heather from below.

"Yup. It's still warm," Jack said in his Texas drawl. "When did Dr. Heath check in with us?"

"That was about an hour ago. He should be showing up pretty soon," Billy said. "He must have left before sun up."

The Bertram leveled out and gained some speed as it cruised along. Chris wiped some of the water off his face and was thankful for the smooth seas. Not one to get seasick easily, this spot high above the boat was indeed a tempting place for it in choppy water. Bringing the binoculars back to his eyes, he looked toward the rich green foliage of the island on his left. At that moment, he heard the smooth hum of a Cessna 208 amphibian aircraft.

Dr. Randy Heath, having zeroed in on the Bertram with his satellite instruments, broke through the clouds at six hundred feet. He was hoping his instruments were right or he would be diving into the volcanic peaks of New Guinea. Chris looked skyward just as the aircraft appeared from the clouds and smiled at the beauty of the moment. It appeared as a great bird popping out of a fog in full motion.

"Awesome," he said to himself.

"Look, Dad," R.O. shouted and pointed to the aircraft.

"Right on the money!" Jack responded.

"I knew that boy could fly, but he's outdoing himself," Billy chimed in.

Heath pointed the Cessna into the wind and found a spot on the edge of the lagoon near the island to land. Within two minutes, the airplane was splashing down in the lagoon during the mild tropical rain. Billy Fly pointed the *Desert Sailor* toward the Cessna and was soon riding its wake toward the beach. Heath killed the motor when he decided he had reached a shallow spot about six feet deep. He opened the back door and heaved a sea anchor out to drop to the sandy bottom. Knowing that the

Bertram couldn't come in that shallow, he took off his shirt, stuffed it inside a waterproof plastic duffel bag full of gear, and sealed it. Tossing it into the water, he closed the side door of the airplane and stepped off the pontoon into the warm sea. He swam toward the boat about one hundred yards away. Chris had climbed down from his perch and tossed a life ring and rope to Heath as he neared the boat. He was soon aboard and toweling dry as best he could in the rain trying to get the saltwater out of his hair.

"Greetings, mates," he said. "Do I smell food cooking?"

"You certainly do," Mavis answered, appearing from below. "Will your plane be safe here?"

"Yes, we're pretty far away from the shipping lanes, and only tourists come to this area to dive or fish. There are no pirates on this end of New Guinea. Although I can't say that about the Indonesian side of the big island. We would have to carry an arsenal with us over there," Heath said.

"Well, we don't need that complication," Jack chimed in.

"Dead fish ahoy!" Chris shouted from the stern of the boat. "I can't believe I sat up there for two hours and saw nothing and now that I'm down here, I spot something.

Billy turned the boat into the stream of dead fish and cruised along at five miles per hour.

"Everybody keep an eye out," directed Jack.

Jack, Chris, R.O., and Randy all lined the sides of the Bertram as it slid carefully along the coastline about two hundred yards off the beach.

"Look over there," Randy said, pointing to an opening in the rainforest.

"A freshwater stream. It's not a pipeline after all, just a freshwater outlet into the sea. The pollution must be coming from somewhere on the island," replied Jack.

"Well, I'm too hungry to dive so let's eat first," Randy suggested.

"Anchors away," Billy said from the helm.

"Sounds good to me. Lunch is ready anyway," Mavis announced at the door of the cabin compartment.

"What's cooking, Mom?" R.O. asked.

"Fish and chips, English style," Mavis answered.

"My favorite," Chris said.

Soon lunch was served and was over quickly.

Billy had taken two M-16s from a closet, which also held three Colt .45s.

"I thought you said there weren't any pirates around here," Jack said.

"Haven't seen any lately, but just in case," Billy smiled and handed Jack a rifle and a pistol.

"Gotcha," Jack replied.

"Anyone for coffee?" Mavis asked.

"No thanks," Billy said as he stepped back out into the rain.

Mavis got up and poured herself a cup of hot coffee, adding cream and two lumps of sugar. When she opened the door of the cabin, she noticed the rain was pouring down heavily again.

"Did it start raining again?" she asked as she stepped onto the bridge from the spiral staircase.

"It never stopped," Billy replied.

"Well, what's on the agenda today for you boys?"

"The fish kill has drifted away so that means the water must be safe to dive in. I think we should dive across the bottom to check for dead invertebrates and head into the small stream from the island. From there, we should go inland to see if we can locate the source," Chris recommended.

"My plans exactly," Randy said as he stepped out of the cabin onto the bridge with a cup of coffee in his hands. "Your dad is below deck refilling the tanks right now."

"Well, I better go get some food for you to take or you won't be able to make the swim into shore or take a short hike in the rainforest. Chris, you did pack your survival bag, I hope?" asked Mavis.

"Sure did, Mom. I don't leave home without it," Chris said with a smile.

Chris handed Randy a utility belt with ropes, expandable water bottle, pocket-size first-aid kit, sun block, cigarette lighter, leather gloves, dry socks in a plastic bag, and two MREs. Randy inserted all of it into his floatable gear bag. The rain poured as they stood under the canopy trying to pack the dry clothes and supplies. Then Chris walked out on the deck wearing only his tropical weight wetsuit, picked up a pair of fins and a regular mask. After he put on the fins, he sat on the gunwale, pulled on the mask, and dropped over the side.

"Where's he going?" Randy asked Jack.

"He's probably going to check water clarity, temperature, I don't know," Jack replied and raised his eyebrows.

Chris had to swim hard to go deep with the wet suit constantly pulling him to the surface. After a few minutes, he swam back to the ladder and tossed his fins in the boat. He climbed on board and went up to the bridge.

"Did you see them?" Billy asked him.

"Yep, just like you said, laying right under the boat," Chris replied.

"See what?" Jack asked as he climbed up the stairs to the bridge.

"Giant manta rays. There are two of them under the boat. Billy said they are fairly common through here, and he spotted them a few minutes ago just after he dropped anchor. I'm surprised the anchor didn't stir them up, but they didn't even move. They're magnificent looking, too," Chris said with an excited expression on his face.

"You know . . ." Jack started.

"I know to be careful because of the spine. Any good diver would know not to swim right over them or within range of the spine. Those big ones could probably stab you at eight to ten feet away," Chris said.

"That's right. They will pull their heads up to get room

to flex their fins, and then they shove the tail up at their intruder," Jack replied. "Under the boat you say. That's very strange."

"That's what I thought. I wanted to check them out before we all got in and they took off from our entry vibrations. We'll probably attract a reef shark with the noise anyway," Chris said.

"I've got some rolls, bagels, and jerky in a bag to take with you. What about water?" Mavis asked as she appeared next to the men.

"We can't drink the stream water even with disinfectant tablets added, so we'll each take a bottle of water. Since it's monsoon season, we'll drain plant leaves to fill them up as we use them," Randy said.

"That's a good plan," added Jack.

"Take a look at these charts," Billy said.

They all crowded around Billy as he laid out a chart of the coastline where they were anchored.

"Here's the *Desert Sailor,* and here's the stream you guys were talking about. It looks like you have about a three- to four-mile hike before the terrain begins to climb dramatically at the base of this old volcano. That's where the topographical markings indicate you'll encounter a waterfall for the stream coming from the highlands. Depending on how clear of a trail you have, it'll take you all day. We better wait until tomorrow morning so we'll have all day to get in and out."

Everyone agreed and settled in for another evening on board the luxury yacht.

The *Desert Sailor* floated calmly in the swells with her passengers totally oblivious to the rumbling of the volcano deep within the rainforest.

11

Beachhead

Jack, Chris, and Randy were geared up on the deck of the *Sailor* under the canopy and ready to go when Jack waved for Billy to come out into the rain.

"What's up?" Billy asked, a tightly woven broad-brimmed Panama hat keeping his head dry but not much else.

"Wrap up a couple of those Colts, and we'll take them with us," Jack answered.

"Good idea," Billy said and proceeded to the bridge where he picked up the two pistols. He went down into the kitchen to find a couple of waterproof bags. With the guns securely protected, he handed one to Jack and the other to Randy.

"Where's mine?" Chris asked as he picked up his mask.

"Mr. Fly needs to keep one in case of an emergency, and I'll let you have one if you need it," his dad responded.

"So it's O.K. for me to carry a Colt Anaconda .44 magnum in Alaska but not a Colt .45 in the South Pacific?" Chris countered.

"Look son, I wouldn't have given you the Anaconda in Alaska but I'm glad you had it under the circumstances. I feel better knowing you can safely use a handgun. But unless there is a need for you to have a weapon, I'll carry it and so will Dr. Heath," Jack said firmly.

"O.K.," Chris said and smiled. "For now anyway."

"Are you guys through dueling over the pistol?" questioned Randy.

"No dueling, just me instructing. Time to go. Do you have a satellite telephone with you?" Jack asked.

"Yes, it's in the sealed duffel with all of our clothes for the trek inland. My experience with New Guinea is that unless there's a village nearby that uses a trail fairly often, it'll be like swimming upstream to find the source," Randy said and fastened the buckle on his buoyancy compensator vest.

"Maybe we'll get lucky," Chris said.

"How about a kiss for good luck," Mavis yelled from the cabin door, not wanting to get in the rain.

"Sure, Mom," Chris replied and stepped toward her. As she leaned forward to kiss him, he grabbed her arms and yanked her into the rain soaking her instantly.

"Payback is going to be rough, big boy," she said and kissed him on the cheek. Turning to her left, she kissed Jack and then just stood in the rain. "What's the rush to get inside?" She parted her hair away from her face and tucked it behind her ears.

The three divers sat on the gunwale and fell backwards into the ocean. Once they were bobbing on the surface, they each rechecked their dive computers and gauges, set their watches, and gave each other a thumbs-up.

"I'm not used to a full mask with a voice microphone," Randy said. "You guys will spoil me."

"Mavis bought them when she knew the kids would be diving off of these atolls. Her nerves were pretty well shot when she watched Chris take off and fly away with everyone on board knowing he would land in a lagoon and take everyone diving," Jack said.

"Hey, Dad, the Italians and the Aussies taught me well. The more flying time I get, the better I'll be," Chris added as he lifted the exhaust hose on his vest and began to descend to a depth of twenty feet.

Soon all three were kicking easily along the sandy bottom of the lagoon.

"Look over here," Randy said. "Empty shells. These mollusks died recently. We're on a trail for sure."

Chris stopped over a small coral head and began to peer inside the small canals. He took out his knife and pried at a piece that chipped off instantly.

"Dead coral?" Jack asked swimming up behind him.

"Sure is," Chris replied.

"This piece is at least twenty years old. What a shame," Jack said.

"Looks like the bottom hollows out for the freshwater runoff of the stream," Randy said.

"Yea, you can see the mixture of the salt and freshwater just ahead," Jack said.

"That is so amazing," Chris added quickly. "It looks like a transparent veil or curtain as the two types of water mix. There's a weird magnification about it."

"Marine life will look bigger, so don't let it fool you," Randy said. "I once saw a nurse shark near the southern tip of New Guinea where the river dumps into Auckland Bay in the Solomon's. It looked to be fifteen feet long but wasn't near that big."

"We had a similar experience with the kids when they were little. We were snorkeling at an inlet on the Yucatan Peninsula of Mexico called Xelja; you know shell ha with the Mayan spelling. We happened across a school of parrotfish that looked about four feet long each. First, I didn't know they even got that big, and second, I've never known them to school," Jack said.

"I remember that, Dad. Wasn't there somebody out there you gave your snorkeling vest to, a woman who had a leg cramp or something?" Chris asked.

"Good memory, son. That's why I always wear a vest,

diving or snorkeling. It can save your life or someone else's," Jack said.

"Here's where we turn, fellas," Randy said in his down-home accent.

"We'll follow you," Jack replied.

"More dead invertebrates," Randy noticed. "This is a hot trail."

"I keep looking for fish, but it seems that last night was the most recent bunch of floaters. The timing aspect of this is quite confusing, for sure," Jack said.

"If there's no pipeline, then someone is controlling the dumping," Chris added.

"Here's the direct stream. We'll have to surface here. I don't see any planktonic debris or fish larvae. This should be a good breeding spot but it looks sterile," Randy alleged.

"My estimation as well," Jack replied.

They broke surface in about eight feet of water and kicked until they could stand up, suddenly feeling the full weight of their equipment. Randy pulled in the sealed duffel that had been floating behind him on the surface from a thirty-foot cord. As they walked up on the beach, they looked back to the *Desert Sailor* anchored about a quarter mile off shore. Mavis was on the back deck in the rain waving so they waved back. She hurried back into the cabin. R.O. was on the bridge with Billy, and they assumed that Heather was back in her bunk sleeping, which she said she planned to do anyway for most of her trip to the South Pacific islands.

The three divers shuffled under the weight of their tanks to the row of palms that shaded the small beach and began to take off their equipment. Dressing under the shade of the big leaves, they put their clothes on and stowed away their scuba gear under the same large bushes before again stepping into the rain.

"No staying dry around here," Chris said.

"No. You guys came just at the beginning of the monsoon

season. I guess you already know that," Randy replied and tied the laces on his hiking boots.

Jack and Chris only had standard athletic shoes, having left all of their heavy hiking gear back at the resort.

"Let's stay on the bank of the stream for as long as we can," Jack suggested.

"Roger that," Chris said and followed him across the beach to where the freshwater flow entered the lagoon. "This is huge. We would call this a river back home in Texas."

"Right you are. But with the monsoon, the flow has increased dramatically," Randy said.

"I'm guessing that it may be five to eight feet deep in some places," Jack said.

"Five or more," added Randy.

The trio climbed from rock to rock soon realizing that at this pace they wouldn't get far very fast.

"I should go back to the plane and fly over, but I'm afraid in monsoon season I would collide with a volcano coming out of the clouds," Randy said as he jumped to a new boulder. "There aren't any mountains on the way home."

"There's a trail over here," Chris revealed as he stepped from a rock to a small path.

"From the look of the leaves, it was cut in the past couple of weeks. Not unusual for the tribesmen around here. They will cut a path to the beach to collect coconuts," Randy said. "Watch overhead for the brown tree snake, and don't step on any old coconuts because the "small-eyed snake" called the *Ikaheka* likes to live in them. Extremely venomous," Randy alerted.

"Now you tell us," Chris said.

Randy moved forward on the trail brushing away the large leaves of the *Cycad bougainvilleana* tree clustered with a Southern Beech and an acacia. He was constantly looking for anything that moved. The trail followed the streambed, once crossing it on some large boulders, and then continued on the other side. The three adventurers followed it for two hours before encountering extremely heavy foliage and a higher incline on the trail.

"I'm not believing this," Chris said as he wiped his face and eyes. The rain had never let up, and they were constantly being bathed with water that pooled on leaves and dropped to the trail below.

Stepping through an opening in the trail onto a flat surface, they were confronted with an awesome sight.

Looking up, Jack said, "I never imagined this would happen. This must be the waterfall that Billy showed us on the map."

"An underground river coming right out of the rock fifty feet above the trail," Randy observed.

The three just stood and stared at the rushing water pouring from the mountain crevasse and billowing down the side of the old volcano. Chris sat on a large rock, bent over and picked up a piece of yellow plastic.

"I don't imagine any of the indigenous tribes would have yellow plastic in their villages would they?" he asked.

"They would have just about anything that a missionary or trader can carry, and what they can take from an oil drilling site," Randy replied, taking the plastic from Chris. "I think we've found our source, but it's on the other side of this rock face."

"Notice how the soil by the stream is void of any life," Jack examined.

"What's that?" asked Chris suddenly.

"Don't move; it's a small earthquake. They're fairly common in these parts," Randy said.

"Is it plate tectonics or volcanic in nature?" Jack asked.

"Probably both," Randy answered. "There's still a lot of energy built up in these formations. These islands have thousands of small quakes every year."

"Well, what do we do now? This isn't a movie. We can't go through a waterfall and step into some imaginary world," Chris said and sat down again.

"We go around the mountain and find the source,"

Randy declared, not willing to quit. "I've got too much at stake not to find it and stop it."

Without wasting time, the three men began moving south around the base of the old volcano. The rain began to fall much harder. The two Colt .45s were the only things that were dry.

12

People of the Rainforest

As the rain continued to pour, Jack, Chris, and Randy followed the volcano's base through the heavy rainforest. They lost the trail to the dense ferns several times only to stumble onto it a few minutes later.

"Great explorers we would make," Chris joked.

"Hey, I resent that," Jack replied and laughed with him.

"I'm a marine biologist so I have protection from all land-based explorer jokes," Dr. Heath said and stopped on the trail as the earth rumbled again.

"That was a little stronger. We must be getting closer to the source," Jack said.

"I don't know if this is such a great idea," Chris warned. "I mean if it blew, we'd go with it."

"I don't think it's to that stage yet," Randy added.

"So you're a vulcanologist too," Jack laughed.

Chris held his right hand up with the Vulcan hand sign from the *Star Trek* series.

"Live long and prosper," he said, trying to look solemn.

"No, I'm no Mr. Spock. Let's just say I've been around these parts for a few years, and these old dormant chimney stacks aren't good for much more than mining their sulfide vents for minerals," Randy replied.

They slowly continued up the trail as it climbed the side of the mountain. With each step in the spongy surface of the rainforest, more rain seemed to reach through the dense canopy overhead. After walking for an hour, they agreed to rest and eat some of the food Mavis had sent with them. Chris, reaching for his portion, turned and was shocked to see the face of a native tribesman standing on a boulder right in front of him. Chris had not seen or heard the man move to the rock.

"Dad," he whispered.

"What Chris?" Jack said as he bit into a piece of jerky.

"We have a visitor," Randy said softly. "And it looks like he's carrying a poison dart tube so don't move quickly. My guess he has his cousins nearby."

Just as Randy uttered the words, four more small men with tattoos and red paint on their faces stepped out of the rainforest.

"They look like miniature Samburu from Kenya," Chris noted.

"There's nothing miniature about their weapons," Randy said. "This one over here has a shrunken head hanging on his necklace."

"Are they still cannibals?" Jack asked quietly.

The man on the rock replied in plain English.

"Only if white man has tender skin. But your skin look tough. I have to boil you a couple of hours to make you chewable," he said solemnly.

"Yes, they look some tough, especially the young one," another tribesman laughed.

Instantly all of the tribesmen were laughing and smiling. Chris, Jack, and Randy tried to join in but couldn't get into the mood of it with thoughts of a boiling cauldron and flames licking over the top running through their minds.

"I like chicken or shark. Humans give me gas," another tribesman said, and they all laughed harder.

The man on the rock raised his dart gun in the air above his head. The native islanders became quiet, and he spoke in a native tongue to them. They then turned and disappeared into the rainforest as quietly as they had appeared. The first tribesman stayed to speak with Jack, Chris, and Randy.

"I learned English from missionary who came to our village and stayed twenty years. We can now speak English, but we don't care for English ways. We are people of the forest, and this is our home. Why have you come?" he asked firmly. "And we give up eating humans long time ago, I think." He smiled as he stepped closer to Chris and poked his left cheek. Chris smiled back.

"We are scientists, men who study nature. We have come today to find the source of the dangerous water that flows into the streams and oceans, killing anything that touches it," Jack answered slowly.

The tribesman thought about this.

"We are Mendam. We are nature. I know what you are talking about. There is factory hidden from sky inside the mountain. The water from it has hurt many of our people, but no one has come to help us. We sent some of our elders into the mountain to find who is doing this and to reason with them. They never came back," the man revealed. The several layers of paint on his face couldn't hide his sadness.

"We've come to help," Randy assured. "I live on a nearby island, and I want this poison to stop flowing, too."

"I can take you to cave in mountain but I warn you, it is waking from time of rest," the tribesman said.

"Do you have a name?" asked Chris.

"My name not important. What I do more important. That is what I am known for. I raise food for village and for government to buy. In return, we get equipment for our village to make our lives good. Before missionaries come, we not know we were uncomfortable. But learning brings new things to those who want to learn. We have told the government agents about the poisons, but no one is listening," he responded.

"That's because whoever is causing the poison is probably paying the government agents," Randy said. "When's the last time you used that blowgun?"

"Just one day past when I saw lizard high in the trees that would make good meal."

"I was just wondering. I didn't know that any New Guinea tribes used blowguns. They're common on New Britain but not here," Randy commented.

"Mendam use them to kill small animals," he said.

"It's the Amazon tribes that use them to kill large animals," Jack said.

"What is Amazon?" the tribesman asked.

"That's a long story; maybe I'll share it with you when all of this is done," was Jack's reply.

"It's half day walk to opening in mountain so we begin," the native said and started up the path without looking behind.

"I guess we better fall in," Randy said and took after him.

"I need to touch base with your mother and Billy so I'll talk as we walk," Jack said, taking out the phone and pulling it from its plastic bag.

"If you were on a concrete sidewalk, you'd almost look like every other pedestrian in Dallas or Fort Worth," Chris said.

"Hello, Billy, this is Jack. We've made contact with a native islander, Mendam tribe, who is going to lead us to the source of the pollution. When we get there, we'll talk to whoever is running the plant, get the details, and head back," Jack reported.

"Roger that, Jack. We're just hanging out playing games in the cabin. The rain is still pouring down, and the radar shows the sky to be thick for a few hundred miles. Stay dry, and we'll talk again in five hours," Billy said.

"Five hours. That would be seventeen hundred," Jack replied. "And we certainly aren't dry. Goodbye."

Jack put the phone back in its bag and tucked it into his backpack where the Colt was also securely placed. He had lagged behind a little but could still see Chris a few yards ahead. He hurried so he would not lose visual contact in the dense forest. At times, it became quite dark on a cloudy day full of rain and appeared to be near dusk all the time. The animals and insects of the forest seemed to be in constant motion, emitting an orchestra of sounds that only the native islanders could understand fully. To Jack, a zoologist, it was a symphony he had not heard before. Each rainforest has its own unique inhabitants, but all share one thing, isolation from other rainforests. Jack only hoped that time could reverse itself for the Amazon basin, Central Africa, and parts of Central America where humans had invaded the natural habitat and destroyed much of the natural balance.

The long walk seemed to never end with the three foreign adventurers calling for a ten-minute rest stop every hour. Their legs were good for kicking through the lagoon but not climbing up and down constantly through the hills and valleys of the ancient volcano's rainforest. After their fourth rest, the native islander spoke again.

"Fill bottles from the rain coming down tree. It good to drink."

Each of them took their empty containers and held them against the spongy bark of a tree and let the water run in slowly as the rain continued to fall. With water inside his shoes, Chris sat down to pull off his running shoes and take off his wet socks to try to prevent blisters. As he laid the socks on the rock next to him, Jack decided to do the same thing.

"How about you, Randy?" asked Jack.

"My boots are waterproof," he replied with a smile.

"Gee, that's great to know," Chris said.

"Well, I live around here, and I know what island hiking is like. It's not a matter of wearing flip-flops or tennis shoes.

I didn't have the heart to tell you when we were dressing on the beach. I figured you would learn soon enough."

"We are nearly there. I think you say, about twenty or thirty minutes. Yes, I tell time too! I have crops at the rail station at certain time or they won't be bought and taken to Port Moresby to be sold to government," the native tribesman said.

"O.K. Then let's keep going," Jack said as he put his socks and shoes on, got up, and took a long drink of water. He then refilled his water bottle.

As they reached a trail in a clearing, the rain pelted them more ferociously. The men could see only about fifty feet ahead through a veiled mist rising from the rainforest floor. Chris wiped the water from his face only to have it pour onto his head and wash his hair back into his face. Finally, he gave up and watched the back of Randy's boots in front of him. He turned around to his father behind him.

"Dad, you still keeping up?"

"I am indeed," Jack replied and rubbed his hair, pushing water down his back, which he didn't feel. "Don't look up, the rain could hurt your eyes if you stare too long, pounding hard on your cornea."

"I thought about that so I just look forward at Randy's dry boots," Chris said.

"Are you girls still crying about my dry feet?" Randy chuckled. "Well, they were dry as long as we were inside the canopy but out here in the open, they are filling up fast."

"Good. I feel better. Misery loves company," Chris said.

The native islander stopped and turned to them.

"We are here," he said.

Jack, Chris, and Randy looked around but couldn't see anything but a rock wall on one side and the rainforest on the other about two hundred feet across the clearing.

"I don't see anything," Chris was the first to say.

"Follow me," the small man said and walked toward the

rock wall at the base of the dormant volcano. When he reached a stack of boulders and a sharp outcropping, he turned sideways and disappeared into the mountain.

"Wow. Did you see that?" Chris asked.

"I did," Jack replied.

Randy was the first one to the spot.

"There's a small opening just big enough to slide sideways into a cave. What do you think?" He asked, looking at Chris and Jack.

"We've come this far. I'll go first," Jack replied and turned, taking a deep breath. He pulled his chest up and in and just barely squeezed through.

Chris was next, followed by Randy. The darkness was overwhelming as was the sudden increase in temperature. Chris pulled out and flicked on the pocket lighter he carried for just such emergencies.

"Dad, I have a flashlight in my bag," Chris stated and handed his backpack to Jack.

"Me too," added Randy.

In a moment, the two flashlights filled the small cave with light, and the three men looked around for the islander. He was standing next to the opening.

"I stop here," he said and left.

"That was a quick exit," Chris said.

"Could be something to do with the volcano and superstitions," Randy replied.

"And he didn't even let us thank him. Well let's find our way into the main cavern and talk to these people," Jack said as he looked around for an internal exit from the small room. "Over there."

Chris was the closest and stepped into a tunnel that was about ten feet long and opened through another small entrance into a large cavern full of lights and machinery.

"Well, I think we've found our problem source," Randy announced. "That over there is slurry and on the other side is a pile of ore tailings. What we have here is an underground gold mine. The operational entrance must have been over the small rise in the rainforest across the clearing. They would need a place to bring in trucks, equipment, and maybe even fly in."

"No kidding," Chris said.

"He's not kidding, son. This underground operation also explains the factory on Karkar Island. That could be where the final product is taken to ship out to be camouflaged as oil products," Jack said. "Watch your step. These old steps were carved out of volcanic rock."

They started to move downward into the cavern.

"And we do know that toxic waste including cyanide are the byproducts of it," Randy informed. "That's what's killing my pearl bivalves."

"Well, let's go see who's in charge," Jack said.

"Dad, isn't that risky?" Chris asked quickly.

"I don't think so, son. We've discovered their secret, and they know that others can do the same. I mean, look at this place. It's huge," Jack replied.

"I don't know, Jack. Chris has a point. If we go barging in, we might disappear like the village elders," Randy warned.

"O.K., then Chris you stay behind; Randy and I'll go exploring," suggested Jack.

"How about the Colt?" Chris asked. "You have one with Randy, and I can keep the other for insurance."

"That's good thinking, Chris," Randy said and removed the gun he was carrying and unwrapped it from the plastic bag. "You know I'm already drying in this heat," he said and handed Chris the weapon and an extra clip.

"We must be sitting on the caldera of the old volcano, and it wouldn't surprise me if they didn't have a geothermal energy source like they had on the island," Jack said.

"Chris, wait for us in the room next to the outside entrance. If we're not back in one hour, call Billy and tell him to get help. Got it?" Jack asked and handed him the cell phone.

"Got it. Be careful," Chris said and stepped behind a large earth-crushing machine and watched Jack and Randy move farther into the mine.

"Ahead on the right. An armed guard," Randy cautioned.

"I see him. It's just like a diamond mine. Can't let the help walk away with the profits," Jack said.

"You mean the slaves," Randy replied.

"More than likely," Jack said when suddenly an alarm siren began to screech.

Four men seemed to come out of nowhere and surrounded them, pointing AK-47 automatic rifles at their chests. Soon a tall man wearing khakis, a shoulder holster with a Beretta 9mm pistol, and tall boots up to his knees walked into the circle. He motioned for the guards to lower their weapons.

He had steel-rimmed glasses and a long mustache that covered his upper lip and curled around his mouth. He had not shaved for a several days, which gave him a menacing appearance Jack didn't trust. The heat had caused his shirt to hold two days of sweat, and he sported a shaved head that was tanned from the tropical sun. Jack noticed he wore a large ruby ring on his right hand, which rested on the utility belt around his waist.

"What do you gentlemen want?" Jon Nickerson asked rather stoically, adjusting his posture to tower over them.

"I'm Dr. Randy Heath with the Long Island Pearl Company; this is Dr. Jack MacGregor, a zoologist, and we're looking for the proprietor of this mine," answered Randy in a businesslike tone, not knowing what to expect.

"You're looking at him," Nickerson replied.

"And your name, sir?" Jack asked politely.

"Nickerson. What do you want?" he asked again.

"We've been following a trail of toxins through the lagoon on the northeast side of the island that is killing fish as far south as Long Island and New Britain. The trail led up a stream into the side of this mountain and to your mine, sir," Randy said pugnaciously.

"So you say," Nickerson replied, seeming never to blink.

"We do say, and we can prove it now. We want to see your environmental impact papers that were filed with the Papua New Guinea government. We will appeal to them to stop this pollution if you won't do it voluntarily," Jack said, looking the Canadian mining engineer in the face.

"I see," Nickerson said. "Well first let me give you a guided tour so you can be accurate in your description of the activities in our little mine." He motioned for the armed men to step aside. "Please follow me, gentlemen."

For the next thirty minutes, Nickerson strode ahead of them like a tour guide pointing out every piece of machinery and the various methods used in the mine. As he walked by the barracks filled with the noise of people eating, he stopped.

"We house our workers here. We give them more than they would ever see in the world outside. At the end of two years, they'll return to their villages much richer but with nowhere to spend it," he said and turned away.

Randy and Jack walked behind him for a few more minutes when Nickerson suddenly stopped.

"Over here we have the biggest secret of all so stay close behind," he said.

Suddenly the earth began to rumble, and the floor of the cave lifted up and slammed down, knocking the three men to their knees.

"My gosh, Jack. That was the biggest one yet," Randy said excitedly. Two guards ran forward with their guns pointed at the newcomers.

"Not a true earthquake. It seems our mother volcano here is trying to wake up, which is why time is of the essence. Follow me," Nickerson directed as the guards lined up behind Jack and Randy.

They walked toward a stone hallway and into the room

where four men were picking away at a solid vein of gold.

"Would you look at that!" Randy exclaimed.

"I've seen that only one other time in my life, in Africa," Jack said. "It was a bank in an ancient riverbed next to an old volcano."

"This is the same thing, minus the sky," Nickerson said. He reached down on the ground to pick up a handful of gold nuggets and handed them to Jack and Randy.

"Your contribution to cleaning up the pollution you've caused?" Jack asked, defiantly tossing them to the ground.

"That's not a good idea, doctor. I'll tell you what. I need two new workers because I just noticed these two slackers slow down."

Nickerson pulled his gun from his shoulder holster and shot one of the men in the back. He fell dead instantly. He quickly turned and killed another worker as he dropped his pick and tried to run away.

Jack and Randy stepped back in horror.

"In fact, I need two fresh workers because the mine will only be open for one more day anyway. By then, I'll have a million in gold nuggets loaded and ready to go."

"Pick up their axes, and if you don't start working, I'll shoot you," Nickerson said calmly and pointed the gun at Jack's head.

Randy grabbed one and swung hard into the wall of gold. An avalanche of nuggets dropped to the cave floor.

"That's the spirit. I knew these two mates were getting a little tired. You just made me about twenty thousand dollars with one swing. More swings like that and I'll be sure to give you a handful of gold nuggets before I leave. You can contribute them to Greenpeace or some other stupid environmental group," Nickerson laughed as Jack picked up the mining tool.

Jack looked over his shoulder at Nickerson who quickly said, "Don't even think about it. You would die before you hit the floor."

Chris hadn't stayed at the secret entrance of the mine. Instead, he decided to follow his dad and Randy in the shadows. He had watched as Jack and Randy were led into a side tunnel by Nickerson and two guards and listened as they were being taken captive. When he heard the two gunshots, he chambered a round in the Colt .45 and started to run into the rock corridor, but then two guards came out and stood by the door. He considered shooting them and charging in to save Jack and Randy but couldn't be sure if they were already dead or if they would be killed when he rushed the guards. Chris didn't know what to do, so he decided to wait and hope that another earthquake would provide him with the distraction he needed. He knew he couldn't wait forever if he were going to save their lives.

13

Water Everywhere

"Heather, don't you think it's time to get out of bed? It's almost time for supper," Mavis said.

"Mom, I've been up three times today," Heather moaned.

"Mom, Billy wants you up on deck, quick," Ryan hollered from the open door.

Mavis turned and stepped toward the open door and was met with a blast of warm water.

"Still storming, I see," Natalie said as she came back into the cabin drenched.

"And I just dried off," Mavis whispered to herself and took two steps toward the narrow stairway that led to the bridge. "Why don't I just put on my swim suit, tie my hair back, and forget it?"

"Sorry to get you out in the weather again, Dr. MacGregor," Billy yelled over the howling wind. "But we've got visitors." He pointed to a small speedboat circling the *Desert Sailor*.

"Who are they?" Mavis inquired as Ryan bounded onto the bridge and picked up a spare pair of binoculars.

"I can't say. They don't look like pirates. Their boat is too small, and for a speedboat to be out in these parts, it has to be from a larger mother ship of some kind, much bigger than my boat," Billy replied. "I got out my two M-16s and my last Colt .45. I also keep a shotgun in the compartment next to the wheel in case I get surprised by intruders at night."

"Who are they?" Heather asked as she stepped onto the bridge and was soaked to the bone in only three seconds. Natalie was right behind her wearing a rain poncho that wasn't much use.

"Hi, honey. Mr. Fly doesn't know," Mavis replied.

Looking through the binoculars, R.O. alerted, "They're moving toward us now."

Billy took the binoculars from Ryan and confirmed it.

"The circling is over. I assume you know how to use one of these?" Billy asked and handed the pistol to Mavis who loaded a round in the chamber.

"I do. I learned when I moved to Texas," she replied.

"Mom, what's happening?" Heather asked worriedly.

"We don't know. These people are getting just a little too close so Mr. Fly wants to be prepared," responded Mavis.

"Gotta gun for me?" R.O. asked. "I can shoot."

"Not yet, young man," Billy replied focusing on the approaching boat.

"I can shoot," Natalie said quickly.

Billy handed her one of the rifles.

When the speedboat got to within fifty yards, two men began to wave out from under the canvas canopy each wearing a big smile.

"They look friendly," Heather said.

"They do act that way," Mavis replied and held her gun low enough that it couldn't be seen.

"I wouldn't trust them," Billy added as he continued looking through the binoculars.

The rain beat down harder, and the island disappeared from view. The speedboat was now only thirty yards away, and the men were still waving and smiling. Billy handed

R.O. the binoculars and held his M-16 just below the instrument panel of the bridge as the boat pulled within twenty-five yards. R.O. was again looking through the binoculars.

"Hey, Mr. Fly, there's someone in the back of the boat, and they're messing with a square, no, make that a cylinder of some kind. He's picking it up," R.O. made known.

Billy picked up the microphone to the Bertram's external p.a. system and flipped a switch.

"Stop, halt, alto," he yelled into the microphone as his voice boomed across the water, becoming lost in the falling rain.

Suddenly a gunshot ripped through the bridge just missing Mavis. Natalie hit the deck in one quick motion. Heather landed on top of her.

"Get down," Billy yelled as he aimed the M-16 and sent four rounds toward the speedboat as it ran up to the side of the *Desert Sailor.*

One of the men in front slumped forward, but another man with the black cylinder stood up and tossed the object into the back of the boat. Billy fired a slew of rounds as the speedboat pushed down the throttle and began to zoom away. He thought he hit a second man in the back seat as the rain covered their escape.

"Bomb on board," Billy yelled just as the explosion went off sending wood, fiberglass, and metal shards everywhere. He hit the deck of the bridge next to Mavis, Heather, and R.O. as the *Desert Sailor* heaved forward in the lagoon. Petrol lines ruptured, and a ball of flame roared across the deck toward the bridge.

Heather screamed, and R.O. leaned up to take a look before Mavis jerked him back down.

"Ryan, stay down," she yelled.

Natalie pushed him down from the other side.

The monsoon swiftly put out the fire as the sea rushed into the back of the boat. Billy was already up and reaching for the emergency duffel he kept under the bridge console. He stuffed the M-16 into it and grabbed for the Colt in Mavis's hand, which he threw in quickly. As the boat began to sink, he pushed open a side panel where two small bottles of Spare Air cylinders were hanging next to six diving masks.

"Everyone grab a mask. Mavis, take a bottle of air. Here are the life vests," he said as he opened a third compartment and threw out the inflatable vests. "Now listen, we're in fifty feet of water. The beach is a quarter mile away. We can easily swim it. I don't think they'll come back since I hit two of them. Wait," he turned and grabbed a compass that was hanging from an instrument panel toggle switch and lifted up the seat in the captain's chair revealing a GLOCK 9mm pistol. "That's my extra in case I ever lost electricity, and the GLOCK shoots in the water," he informed. He hung the compass around his neck with its nylon cord lanyard and stuffed the GLOCK inside the band of his shorts. "We swim southeast to the beach. O.K., get ready to get wet," he said.

"We're already wet," Heather replied as the water reached halfway up to the bridge.

"Let's go now. I'll pull the duffel. It's sealed," Billy said and jumped into the ocean holding onto his mask and duffel.

"Go, Ryan," Mavis yelled and R.O. jumped in hurriedly. Natalie followed him in.

"I'm going," Heather shouted and followed her.

Mavis went in last as they kicked hard to clear all the wires and parts of the sinking cruiser. They swam for about three minutes before Billy stopped and began to inflate his vest and pull out the GLOCK. They all followed his lead. Mavis kept looking around for her two children and Natalie the entire time. When they turned to look at the boat, all that was visible was an antenna protruding a few feet out of the water.

"I'm glad I've got insurance," Billy smiled. "Let's get moving before it gets darker. That would create a different problem."

The five swam as best they could without fins and with their clothes on. Billy had warned them not to take off anything they would need for the island. Every few minutes they would pass around the spare bottle of air, a safety device divers use, so that everyone could get a deep breath.

An hour passed and they still couldn't see the island because of the heavy rain.

"Mr. Fly, are you sure we're going in the right direction?" Mavis asked.

"Sure am. We should see it any minute," Billy replied.

"There it is," Heather shouted.

"Ditto that. It's an island for sure," Natalie said in relief.

"I'm looking at the bottom, Mom. It's only about ten feet deep here," R.O. said.

Within a few minutes, they were all standing up and walking the last fifty yards to the beach. The rain had not let up so they kept their masks on so they could see. Once on the beach, they gathered under a canopy of palm trees that appeared to be growing out of one main trunk. The giant leaves partially blocked the pouring rain.

Heather was the first to sit down on the beach. Mavis slumped down next to her and watched Billy Fly drag the duffel up to the partially protected piece of sand. Ryan just stood and looked around. Billy finally sat down.

"Not bad for an old man," Billy said and took a deep breath.

"I'm impressed, Billy," Mavis said and wiped water from her lips as Heather began to wring it out of her long blonde hair. "You were really prepared for the attack."

"One can't call fire and rescue out here. You are all on your own. I swim for an hour a day to stay in shape. I have the same safety gear arrangement on the lower deck. There's a large escape hatch over the forward bed with survival equipment in a duffel down there too," he replied. "However, I did let that boat get too close. I should have hailed and shot him sooner."

"You've got three rifles hidden on the boat?" R.O. asked as Billy pulled the M-16 out of the duffel.

"No, I have two rifles and a shotgun. But I have masks and vests stowed just about everywhere."

"I've never used these spare bottles of air before," stated Mavis. "Jack says that if you're a good diver, you'll always keep track of your dive and you'll never need them."

"I guess he's right. But sometimes equipment fails, and I don't want to take that chance and be that one in ten thousand statistic," Billy replied.

"Convinced me," Mavis answered. "When we get back, I'm buying five of them."

"Mom. Pretty soon we'll have a hundred pounds of equipment to dive with," Heather complained.

"But don't you love the new masks I bought. Oh my!" Mavis put her hands to her mouth. "Two of my new five hundred dollar masks are still on the boat."

"Don't worry, doc. We'll go salvage everything later, and I'm insured. I'll call for help." Billy pulled his cell phone out of the duffel and poured water out of it.

"I don't suppose it's waterproof?" Heather asked.

"About as waterproof as the one you dropped in the toilet," R.O. laughed.

"You know I had it rolled in the band of my shorts and forgot about it," Heather said defensively.

"Stop it guys," Mavis jumped in. "I don't want a child-induced headache while stranded on a tropical beach without coffee."

"I dropped mine in a swimming pool last summer, Heather. So it happens to all of us," Natalie said.

"Polynesian roast is all I've got." Billy declared as he took two packs of freeze-dried instant coffee from the duffel and produced a tin cup that would be the makeshift coffee pot. He next pulled out a plastic box of matches. "One never knows how long we're going to be a guest on one of these small islands," he stated with a smile.

"Oh no," Heather said as she watched him take out a handful of freeze-dried food and jerky. "I don't do freeze-dried food. I got plenty of that in East Africa," Heather commented.

"Other than a spare pair of flip-flops, that's about it," Billy replied and sat down next to Mavis. "You folks don't seem too upset about the pirates and the bomb going off."

"Billy, we're upset, but when you start adding up all we've been through the last six months, we know that there are bad people out there who want to stop good people like you and my husband Jack. We know we just have to keep moving on. We can't let them control our lives. A cup of coffee makes me feel normal, and the kids watching me drink it makes them feel normal and assured that their mom hasn't lost her cool," Mavis stated dryly.

"You are all very brave," Billy added.

"Thank you. Now kids, find some dry wood," instructed Mavis.

"Mom, I've got water pouring down my shorts," R.O. said. "I guess I don't need a bath tonight."

"That's not even funny, Ryan," Heather rolled her eyes.

"If you'll look under some of those big leaves on the ground, you might find some dried coconut shells. They burn pretty good," Billy informed. "But watch out for snakes. This island has several venomous species."

"That does it for me," Heather said and stood up.

"And where are you going, missy?" Mavis demanded in her strongest British accent.

Heather just looked at her and sat back down.

"R.O., come with me. We'll find something that'll burn," Billy said and got up, pushing the water out of his long white hair now touching his shoulders.

"I'll go too," Natalie added and hopped up dusting the sand off her backside.

After about fifteen minutes of foraging up the beach, R.O., Natalie, and Billy Fly came back with some sticks wrapped in palm leaves to keep them dry. The air was so damp that it took several tries before a fire would start and last for more than a minute. R.O. kept bringing more needed fuel until the fire was two feet across and about eight inches high off the sand. Fresh rainwater for the coffee was drained from the pools on the leaves of large tropical plants next to the beach. Thirty minutes later, Mavis was drinking a cup of strong black Polynesian roast coffee from one of six Styrofoam cups that Billy had in his all-producing duffel bag.

"This is so good," Mavis said, savoring the taste.

"Mom, you are so addicted," Heather said.

"Yes I am, dear. Caffeine will do that to you," Mavis agreed. "But studies show . . . "

"I'm not interested in scientific studies," Heather shot back.

"So, you're not interested in what your father does?" Mavis replied.

"Yes. You know what I mean. Don't twist my words around," Heather argued.

"Mom," R.O. whispered from beside her.

"What is it, Ryan?" Mavis snapped back still irritated with Heather.

"There's a little man standing next to the tree, and he has a little head hanging around his neck," R.O. whispered again.

"I swear, Ryan O'Keefe MacGregor. When we get back to Gloucester, I am going to fine you more than the worth of the Crown Jewels and make you write the longest paper you have ever written. I mean it will be twenty pages long and . . . you're right. He is little. I see the head." Astonished, Mavis's jaw dropped.

"Wow," whispered Natalie.

"Don't move too quickly," Billy warned, slowly standing up.

Heather just stared as four more men appeared beside him.

"Have you seen three men come from this beach today?" Billy asked them.

"Can they speak English?" Heather inquired.

"Some can. Missionaries did it," Billy said and looked at the five native islanders.

"Yes. We can," one of them answered.

"They do speak," Heather said.

"And yes, we walk, eat, and occasionally read book," one of the tribesmen said and stepped forward.

"Can you tell us where they are?" Billy asked. It was growing darker all around them.

"They went into mountain to find ones who poison ocean," the native islander replied.

Mavis stood up and asked, "Can you take us to them?"

"Yes, it long walk and night is here," he responded.

"He's right. That's a pretty thick jungle in there, and we'd need torches to travel at night," Billy informed. "It's almost impossible now."

"We want to help. We want to stop poison. You have fire. We build torches," the native islander said. He then spoke in his native tongue to the other men who fanned out and started gathering the needed materials for torches. Before long, each person had a long branch with dried matted material wrapped in split green bark.

"Follow us closely so not get lost at night," the native islander said.

Mavis took one last big swig of her coffee and dropped the cup on the beach next to the litter they had produced. She then reached down, picked up all the trash, and put it in one pile.

"I'll get it later," she said and smiled at Natalie.

Billy slung the M-16 over his shoulder and put the GLOCK in his shorts pocket. He tightened the waist drawstring to keep the added weight from pulling off his shorts. He handed the .45 to Mavis, and she tucked it under her nylon belt. Ryan glanced repeatedly from the human head hanging from one of the men's neck to the face of the man who kept grinning at him with big white teeth.

They started out in a single-file line, walking up the beach for about ten minutes before they entered the rainforest on a narrow two-foot-wide path. It looked well traveled and was free of normal forest overgrowth.

Mavis talked to the kids to keep them focused on the journey rather than the elements around them. Natalie just followed along quietly. Wearing only deck shoes and lightweight tennis shoes, they resisted complaining because the native islanders were all barefoot. The rain never stopped, and each would continually wipe water from their faces. Eventually they grew accustomed to water running down their backs, through their shorts, and down their legs.

The hours passed quickly. The native islanders would stop to let them rest for a few minutes as they began the uphill climb on the narrow path at the base of the volcano. The torches continued to burn without much of a flicker.

"What was that?" Heather asked.

"It's a small tremor," Billy replied.

"Earthquake? Mavis asked.

Then another tremor, larger than the last, hit and shook the trees all around them.

"Wow, that was a big one," R.O. said and looked at the native islander behind him. "Can I wear that?" he asked.

The man smiled. He took off the shrunken head and draped it around R.O.'s neck.

"Let's keep going," Billy hurried. "We've got to find them soon. It's getting close to midnight, and who's to say if they might be in trouble. Obviously the men who blew up my boat knew we were out there."

"I agree. I just didn't want to alarm the kids so I didn't bring it up. It's always been on my mind," Mavis said.

The downpour got heavier and heavier. Each step on the spongy vegetation of the rainforest trail seemed to bog them down more and more. No one complained any longer. It wouldn't have mattered. Each knew the importance of moving forward. Two more hours passed in the darkness and the rain.

"We are close to entrance in mountain," one of the islanders said.

"Entrance to the mountain?" asked Mavis.

"Yes. We showed them the way to the factory hidden in the mountain," he replied.

"We better hurry," Billy warned and pushed his wet hair back from his face.

"I think I'm getting a blister on my right foot," Heather announced and sat down on the soaked ground to take off her tennis shoe. "Yup, it's a blister all right."

One of the native islanders stepped forward, stripped a long skinny leaf from a plant and bent down, wrapping it around his foot three times. He then pointed to Heather's foot.

"I get it," Heather replied.

He handed her another long leaf, which she wrapped in the same way and put back on her shoe.

"That feels better. Thank you," she said and smiled.

"You're welcome," the islander replied with a bigger smile. "It heal your foot."

"That's amazing," added Natalie.

"Let's go," Billy interjected as the lead islander moved forward in the rainforest with them all behind him.

When they reached the clearing, the rain seemed to be coming down harder. Water sloshed around their feet as they moved toward the straight rock face at the base of the volcano. One by one, the torches finally began to soak up the water and extinguish until there was only one left. Sheltered by a rock outcropping, they all gathered in a small huddle, including the islanders.

"Follow the passageway to inside. That where we left them," the leader explained.

"Thank you," Billy said and offered his hand.

The islander shook his hand and turned to leave.

"Wait," Mavis said quickly. She reached over and took the human head on a string from around R.O.'s neck. "You forgot something."

"Oh, Mom. That is so cool," R.O. whined.

"That, young man, is for their culture, not ours," Mavis firmly stated and grimaced a bit as she handed over the head.

As the tribesman took it, he smiled. "This is my grandfather's greatest enemy. We don't take heads anymore. Too messy," he smiled.

"Thank you and that's good," Mavis replied with a grin.

"Thanks for letting me wear it," R.O. said with a tone of sadness in his voice.

The islanders turned and walked into the sheets of rain that were still falling. Mavis caught another big drop on the end of her nose and decided she would give up wiping away the water.

"Mom, why bother?" Heather asked.

"I agree. Mr. Fly, after you," Mavis said and they stepped into the opening in the side of the mountain.

The earth shook beneath their feet.

14

The Devil's Breath

The sweat rolled off Chris's forehead into his eyes. The burning sensation caused him to wake suddenly. He accidentally hit himself in the head with the Colt .45, forgetting he was holding a gun. Puzzled, he looked at his watch. He had been asleep for three hours. His heart began to race. "How could this have happened?" he thought to himself. He again wiped the sweat off his brow and took a deep breath to shake off his sudden shock of learning he had fallen asleep. He was very hot.

He knew the temperature in the mammoth cave had to have risen well into the nineties as his clothes were soaked with perspiration and sweat was running down his legs. He leaned forward on his knees and looked toward the cave tunnel where he had last seen his dad and Randy. The guards were gone. His heart began to race faster. He looked again at his watch. It was near midnight. He heard a noise to his right next to the mechanical slurry and trained the gun in that direction, blinking to remove a drop of sweat on his eyelashes.

"Natalie," he whispered as he saw Natalie, Mavis,

Heather, R.O., and Billy Fly walking through that part of the cave toward him.

He sprang to his feet, stepped from his hiding place, and scanned the cave for guards. No one was in sight. He took off in a run down a short incline sidestepping some equipment and began to sprint toward the group.

"Look, it's Chris," R.O. announced loudly.

"Hey, Chris," Heather joined.

Thinking about the guards with the guns, Chris felt chills running up and down his spine. Twenty feet away and still on the run, he patted his free hand over his mouth and ran by them.

"Let's go," he said in a whisper, but loud enough for everyone to hear.

"Move quick," Billy instructed, getting the message. "Don't talk."

Mavis grabbed R.O. and put her right hand over his mouth as he started to say something. She dragged him along with her left hand under his right shoulder. Natalie was the first to catch up to Chris as he ducked behind a large mining machine. When Chris stopped, she threw her arms around his neck tight.

He was trying to catch his breath.

"What happened?" he asked in a whisper as everyone gathered close to him.

Natalie released him, and Mavis stepped in close.

"Some pirates sank the boat, and the native islanders led us to the cave," Mavis said softly, reaching out to point her right index finger at R.O. who had started another sentence.

"Who were they?" Chris asked. "No, don't answer that. I have a feeling I know. They were the same ones who took Dad and Dr. Heath."

Mavis let out a moan but quickly caught herself.

"Where are they?" she questioned anxiously.

"I don't know. They were in a tunnel down the way, and

then when I woke up, they were all gone," Chris said.

"You fell asleep and let them take Dad," Heather said in disbelief.

"Look. It's over ninety degrees in here and staying awake after a four-hour hike through the rainforest is nearly impossible," Chris defended.

"We just did that," reminded Billy. "And if I sit down, I'll pass out for ten hours. So everyone cool their jets and get a grip. We've got a problem, and we need to resolve it. I suggest that Chris and I move down through the cave and see if anyone is left in here or if everyone's gone. This place is huge."

"That's a good plan, Mr. Fly," Mavis said. "You have your rifle, and Chris has a .45. Natalie, you go with them and take Mr. Fly's GLOCK with you. I know you can shoot so don't argue. I'll stay here with Heather and Ryan. We'd just be baggage, and if you need to get out on the run, you can run faster than a herd of people."

Billy retrieved the GLOCK from his pocket and handed it to Natalie.

"It's damp, but it'll shoot straight," he said.

"I don't want you all to stay in the cave," Chris advised. "Go back to the entrance and stay next to the rock over-hang. If something happens down here, you won't be trapped. I can only guess the islanders showed you the way. If you have to leave, just head out into the rainforest and make a lot of noise. They'll find you."

"Kids, let's go," Mavis said and began moving in the shadows of the machinery as she led them back to the tunnel to the outside world. Glancing back, Heather waved and then hurried on behind R.O.

"Lead the way, boss," Billy said to Chris.

"Stay five feet behind each other so one bad guy can't take us all out with one shot," Billy said. "Warrior instincts never leave a man."

Chris walked slowly toward a giant trailer of crushed

rock and then toward a stack of drill pipe that seemed oddly out of place.`

"What's that over there?" Natalie whispered. "It's huge."

"It's a rock grinder. Works like a big tooth drill; it takes chunks of rock off a wall and breaks it up. Then miners come behind it and check out the deposits," Billy answered.

Chris held up his hand for them to stop. Natalie brushed her wet hair away from her face as sweat ran down her shirt.

"Two men running down the cave. They're carrying duffels," observed Chris.

"Looks like everyone is moving somewhere," Billy added.

"The tunnel is just up here, past that building on the left. Those are barracks. When I was down here earlier, there was lots of noise coming from them," Chris said.

"They're pretty quiet now," Natalie commented with sweat running down her side.

"Listen. I'm going to walk slowly past the barracks. Then I'll signal for you both to follow," Chris said and stepped out into the open.

Natalie grabbed him quickly and kissed him on the lips.

"Be careful," she said as she pulled away.

He moved away from the machinery and measured his gait so that he looked like he belonged in the mine, concealing the Colt under his right armpit. As he walked by the barracks, it was completely quiet. He drew closer to the tunnel, turned and waved, moving only a few fingers down on one side of his body. Billy came first with Natalie walking next to him as if they too knew where they were going.

A couple of minutes later, all three were standing next to the tunnel. Chris stepped in first, and Billy and Natalie followed. He held the Colt out in front of him. Billy slung the M-16 down to his side and released the safety. Natalie stood at the rear with the GLOCK pointing toward the opening behind her.

"It's empty," Chris said. "What's this on the floor?"

Billy leaned down, raked up a handful of rocks, and held

them up to the dim light bulbs hanging on a single line around the small room.

"Solid gold nuggets. This handful is probably worth thousands," he said. "It may be top grade. It's no wonder they shut down digging for ore when they struck this vein. I've only seen one other like it . . . well there aren't too many around here."

"Then I know a girl who needs her college tuition paid for," Natalie said, picking up a handful of nuggets and stuffing them in her pockets. "Don't tell me to put them back Chris. This is an illegal mine. And you took the safe off the Japanese ship without asking. You can't tell me this gold isn't mine," she looked away when he looked at her.

As she retrieved a second handful, Chris noticed the two picks on the floor and the pool of blood next to the wall. He couldn't concentrate on the gold for the blood.

"We better keep moving," he said.

"I agree. Your girlfriend and I are set for awhile so let's go find your dad." Billy stuffed his pockets with gold nuggets. "I'm going to use this to help those natives out there and . . . hey, tell me about the safe. What's with that?"

"She's just talking, it's no big deal. I'll tell you about it later," Chris said as he decided to pocket some gold nuggets. Gold fever had struck them all.

"I've got an idea, Mr. Fly. You go back to the cavern entrance and find Mom, Heather, and R.O. I know you're fit but this heat is going to start working on you before it does me. We'll swap weapons. You take the .45, Natalie keeps the GLOCK, and I'll carry the M-16. When you get there, wait until daylight and follow the trail back to the beach. As long as you're going down hill, you're headed in the right direction," Chris directed. The mountain rumbled, and the floor shook. Rocks from around the small room fell off the wall and bounced like rubber balls toward them.

They quickly ran through the short tunnel into the light

of the mammoth cave where they nearly collided with a worker. Fortunately, he didn't see them.

"O.K. I'm headed off to the entrance. You kids don't stay in here too long. Chances are they've already moved Jack and Randy somewhere else," Billy said. "Be careful, and Chris you've got a full clip in the rifle."

Billy hurried back down through the maze of machinery and was lost in the dim lighting as Chris and Natalie turned in the opposite direction.

Waving the GLOCK around, Natalie asked, "Where do we go?"

"Be careful with that. There's a bullet in the chamber, and all you have to do is pull the trigger," Chris warned.

"Chris MacGregor, I know how to shoot a gun. Do I have to go through the whole story again about my grandfather Harry in Carter County, Oklahoma, and all the lessons he gave me?" she responded softly.

"No. It was just a reminder," Chris replied.

As they passed by the area that was stacked with machinery and metal stairs leading to rooms at the top of the mine, the heat grew worse. Both teens were now sweating profusely and needed water, water that was overflowing everywhere outside of the cavern.

"Keep your eye out for a water tank of any kind, hopefully one that isn't polluted," Chris said.

"Right there on that bulldozer. There's a plastic water container," Natalie answered.

They hurried over to the bulldozer, and Chris smiled when he saw the Igloo brand, knowing it was most likely for human consumption. He opened it carefully and peered inside slowly.

"It's half full," he said and put two fingers in and tasted it. "No chemicals."

Then he tipped it over part way and Natalie set the gun on the ground and cupped her hands for a big drink.

"It's warm, but it tastes great," she said and then

splashed a big handful on her face and rubbed off the sweat. Chris drank, he estimated, a quart himself.

"Chris, pour some on my hair to get the sweat out. It keeps running in my eyes," she said.

Chris obliged; then she returned the favor. Thoroughly refreshed, Natalie picked up the gun and followed as Chris continued the trek through the giant cave.

Billy reached the outside entrance and heard R.O. talking to Mavis.

"I'm back. The kids wanted me with you. I'm not as spry as I used to be, and if I had to run, I would hold them up and someone might get hurt," Billy said.

"Where's your rifle, Mr. Fly?" R.O. asked.

"Your brother's got it. I swapped weapons. We're to wait here until daylight, and then try to make our way back to the beach. I figure the little guys will find us once we're on the trail. To us, that's a jungle out there. To them, it's their neighborhood. If a stranger is walking through, they'll notice it." The wind blew a wave of rain on them, soaking all four. "That felt good after the heat inside the cave," Billy declared.

"What time is it?" asked Heather.

Mavis checked her Rolex Explorer.

"It's nearly two in the morning," she said.

"No wonder I'm sleepy," Heather replied.

"But I thought you were Dopey or Grumpy!" R.O. said sarcastically.

"Well since you remember that Disney movie so well, I'm called Doc and can order you back into the mine or anywhere else," Mavis snapped back.

"Gimme five, Mom. Good job!" Heather smiled.

R.O. just stood dumbfounded at being teamed up on as Mavis and Heather slapped hands splashing water in their faces. The temporary smiles felt good too.

"Let's move up against the wall a little more, sit down, and close our eyes," Mavis tiredly said.

"Sounds like a plan," Billy replied, sitting down on the spongy wet ground.

"I was wet with salt water, wet with rain water, dry from volcanic heat, wet from sweat, and wet from the rain again," Heather said as she sat in a puddle of water. "Oh well, it beats the Sahara all to heck."

"Ditto that," R.O. answered from a pool of water two inches deep around him.

"Did I hear you two agree on something?" asked Mavis.

"No, it was the wind blowing," R.O. quipped and leaned against the rock wall, closing his eyes.

Sheets of water ran off the side of the mountain in front of them. They all felt like a giant fan was blowing it at them a few seconds of every minute. Exhausted, the four soon nodded off to sleep.

Chris and Natalie reached the end of the cave where a massive brick wall had been built and had only a metal door entrance.

"Do you feel that heat?" Natalie asked.

"It's going to be really hot in there, but we've got to check it out," replied Chris.

They approached the door and turned to look back down the cave from where they began. It was so dim they couldn't see more than a hundred yards. From this vantage point, the machinery looked like rows and rows of toys scattered in a child's sandbox. Chris touched the metal door.

"It's hot but not enough to burn, so I don't expect flames on the other side," Chris said. "Close your eyes until we see if it is hot on our skin. If we don't feel any pain, then I'll tell you when to look."

"What if someone is on the other side?" she asked.

"That's the chance we'll have to take."

He grabbed the metal handle and pulled; the door opened easily. He looked to the ground and covered his eyes as he stepped in. There was a rush of heat, but it didn't feel worse than a hot sirocco wind.

"Open," Chris said, and they both looked up.

"Oh my gosh," Natalie said quickly.

"This is incredible."

They walked into the cavern, an extension of the other one but cut off so that the gold mine could operate without the intense heat from the small stream of molten magma that flowed on the far side down the wall into an underground vent.

"The lava works its way up the volcanic dome and overflows back to the core through little streams like this. It can't be more than twelve inches wide, but think of all the heat it's producing," Chris said. "It feels like it must be 150 degrees in here."

"Yes, I had a geology professor once tell me that getting bonus points was like retrieving car keys that had been dropped in molten lava. It's not going to happen!"

"Every thing burns in lava, and this brick wall keeps the heat in here like a big kiln. There's the end of the cave. Let's get out of here," Chris said.

The mountain shook again; the floor of the cave moved and lifted up. The brick wall fractured and began to fall.

"Run!" Chris screamed and took off with Natalie behind him.

When they had ran about one hundred feet, they turned and watched part of the brick wall fall to the floor around the door, covering it entirely.

"Chris, we're on the wrong side of the door," Natalie exclaimed.

"How stupid can I be?" Chris asked.

"We are idiots," Natalie replied.

"We have no choice but to go toward the end of the cavern past the lava flow. Protect your eyes. We're a hundred feet away but that's thousands of degrees," Chris said.

The two walked hurriedly through the immense heat to the dark end of the cave and met a dead end. Steam was rising through the cave toward the ceiling. Chris looked up.

"There's got to be a vent up there for all this heat to get out or it would be two hundred degrees in here," Chris said.

"There's no way for us to climb up there; we've got to go back and try to dig our way out brick by brick," Natalie suggested. "And I feel like I could faint."

Chris agreed and they walked quickly back to the pile of bricks covering the door. They worked for nearly thirty minutes before they had to stop from the heat and the blisters on their hands. They leaned against the pile and sat down.

"Not a smart place to sit," Chris cautioned, and he looked at Natalie.

"You're right. Wait, I feel a tremor coming on now." They both jumped up and ran as fast as they could, with Chris scooping up the rifle and the pistol from the cave floor.

"What's happening? I don't feel the vibration as much but it's still there," Natalie asked and looked at Chris who was as red in the face as she was from the heat.

A booming noise echoed through the cave. The brick wall next to where the door was began to fall again. But it wasn't an earthquake. A large yellow earth-moving machine pushed through from the other side, climbing the fallen pile of brick. Inside the steel cage was Billy Fly grinning from cheek to cheek when he saw the two kids. He drove the Caterpillar over the brick and stopped next to them.

"Need a lift?" he asked.

Natalie and Chris quickly climbed up on the big machine and inside the driver's protective cage. Billy shifted the massive gears and reversed it with the two sticks that controlled the tracks on each side. It jerked forward until it was in a steady climb back up the pile of bricks and over and into the next room. He continued driving until they reached the barracks. Once there, Billy stopped, leaving the engine running.

"What made you come back?" asked Natalie.

"I couldn't leave you kids down here by yourselves. I might not be able to run very fast, but I can shoot the eye out of a coconut at one hundred yards," he replied and smiled.

"What's the eye of a coconut?" Natalie asked. "I've heard that before."

"It's the dark spots on the outside," Chris rapidly answered.

"Oh, a good shot," Natalie said and smiled. "You're as good as Gwennie."

"What's that old gal been telling you now?" Billy questioned.

"She could do that same trick," Natalie said.

"Well, the truth is she can, and she's a darn good aviator too!" Billy exclaimed.

"Now what?" Natalie inquired.

"When I was coming to find you, I spotted a shaft running behind the barracks. We'll go there first. That's got to lead somewhere," Billy responded.

"Well, we're glad you came after us," Chris said. "Thanks."

"I fired this up when I came into the cave since we hadn't spotted anyone on the first trip. When I saw the wall collapse around the door, I didn't know if you were on the other side, but I just had a gut feeling you were," Billy said. "I had to wait to be sure the pile of bricks was stable. It gets real hot down here doesn't it?"

"Too hot. Let's get to the barracks," Chris replied.

They drove to the barracks and entered through the door that faced the tunnel of gold nuggets. Reaching the barracks, Billy killed the engine, and the three exited the Caterpillar. Once inside, they looked around at the rows of bunks, a smelly latrine, and a poorly stocked kitchen.

"Looks like slave quarters to me," Natalie was the first to say.

"It just occurred to me that if everyone is gone, then the electricity might be the next thing to go. We've got to find lanterns or something fast," Billy advised.

"Let's keep going toward the guards' quarters. They've got to be better than this," Chris said.

After ten more minutes of rummaging through rooms, they found the guards' room with individual beds, cool air coming through ceiling vents, and a cafeteria, which had a fresh salad bar.

"Look, a cooler." Natalie walked over to it and stood in the doorway of the frozen food locker. Goose bumps ran all over her body. "The chill is really, really refreshing."

Billy and Chris joined her, and the cold air invigorated them. Chris spotted a gallon of milk; he unfastened the plastic lid and poured the liquid into his mouth, letting it run down the side of his face and neck.

"Save some for an old man," Billy said, and Chris handed him the jug.

"I'll settle for some orange juice." Natalie opened a quart carton of the juice.

"I feel bad for your family out in the rain," Natalie said.

"Don't worry about them, the little guy with the head around his neck showed up. We had all fallen asleep, and when I looked up, he was two feet from my face. He said he would walk them back to the beach at daybreak. I imagine that he had never lost sight of us. That made the decision to come after you much easier. We need to move on."

As Chris turned, he saw a row of caps hanging on hooks on the wall. He walked over and started going through them until he found a clean one. He shoved his hair back from his forehead and put it on.

"Got one for us?" Natalie asked as she and Billy approached.

Before long, all three had on caps, pulling their nasty hair from their faces. Natalie opened a row of cabinets on one wall.

"Clean uniforms," she said.

All three of them looked at the official shirt and realized their importance. Soon they had found a size that fit and had changed into clean shirts that had the company's mining logo above the right pocket and "Security" printed over the other.

"Flashlights," Billy announced from across the room when he opened a cabinet on the wall.

Armed with clean shirts, flashlights, weapons, and food in their stomachs, they headed down the hallway away from the barracks. Just then, the electricity failed and the lights went out.

"Well, we made it just in time," Natalie said as the mountain began to shake. They stood still trying to maintain their balance.

The quake lasted for three full minutes, the longest so far.

"We better hurry and find Jack and Randy before this whole mountain goes up like a Roman candle," Billy suggested.

Even in the darkness with only their flashlights, they picked up the pace. In a few hours, the sun would begin to rise and the monsoon would fall even harder.

15

The Gloucester Rocket

At 7:00 A.M., Adi charged through the door with a worried look on her face. Young Deer paused from his daily duty of checking the manpower list for the resort and the proposed dining room menu for the next week. As Billy Fly's partner, he took an active role in as much of the management as possible. He was also in charge of the marina.

"Bill, I'm worried. Billy hasn't radioed in since yesterday," Adi said and paced in front of the big window overlooking the seventy-five-boat marina.

"Could be they're having fun or exploring a new reef. There could be lots of reasons," Young Deer replied.

"I don't buy that. Billy Fly has never failed to call me every day when we're apart since the day we got married. He wouldn't forget now. I called Barbara, you know, Dr. Heath's wife, and she said she hasn't heard from him either. I called the pearl company, and Roosevelt said he doesn't know where they are. Who's left to call?" she asked, showing her frustration.

"Let me call Cody in Honolulu to see if he's got any ideas," Bill answered.

"O.K., but please do it right away. Thank you," Adi said and left.

Young Deer walked across his large office and sat down behind a mahogany desk covered with a mixture of items ranging from several Polynesian tribes to his own Cherokee tribe back home in Oklahoma. He glanced at the world clock on the wall and could see that it was eleven o'clock in the morning in Honolulu. The line rang through.

"High Seas Security, may I help you?" the voice answered.

"Yes, this is Bill Hill down here on New Britain; is Cody Bridwell in this morning?" Bill asked.

"Hi, Bill, this is Sheila."

"Hi, Sheila, I didn't recognize your voice right away."

"When are you coming back to Hawaii? You still have my number, don't you?" she asked.

"Sure do and you can expect to hear from me when I'm there next month. There's a resort convention I need to go to very soon. Now where's Cody, this is kind of an emergency."

"I'll look forward to it. I'll get him for you. Later." Bill heard two beeps as she transferred the call to Cody Bridwell.

"Cody," he answered.

"Hi, Cody, this is Bill."

"Hey, man, when are you coming my way?" Cody asked jovially.

"Next month."

"You made quite the impression on Sheila. She didn't stop talking about you for weeks."

"I gathered that when I just talked to her. Hey," Bill said sharply. "We've got an emergency down here and need some help. Billy and some guests haven't called back from an adventure trip out toward the Admiralties and Papua New Guinea. Billy had a local pearl company employee, Dr. Randy Heath, and Dr. Jack MacGregor and his family on his boat. We can't contact them."

"That's not Jack MacGregor the famous zoologist, is it?" Cody asked.

"Yes, it is," Young Deer replied.

"That's not good. He's made quite a few enemies on both sides with his stand on some environmental issues, and any one of them would like to see him disappear," Cody responded. "Some want him to be more extreme while others want him to be more moderate. Sounds like a logical guy to me. I've even heard about it among my security friends here in Hawaii in case he came our direction or stayed on the Pacific Rim a few more months. He made our VIP security list of people to look out for."

"What can we do?" Young Deer asked.

"I've got assets in Port Moresby," Cody responded.

"Port Moresby? I'm one of your shareholders and didn't know that," an astonished Young Deer said.

"There are some things you don't want to know, trust me. We serve as the private security force for most of the United Nations and Australian delegates that go to Indonesia. Seems the Indonesian government doesn't hold a neutral view when it comes to protection. I'll fire up the new Dassault Falcon 7X and meet you at Cape Gloucester in four hours. It can cover the 3,600 nautical miles at .80 mach. That will give my team in Port Moresby time to organize a search and retrieve mission. Where were they last sighted?" Cody asked.

"They were headed to Karkar Island," Young Deer replied.

"That's gold mining country, isn't it?"

"Yes, it is."

"I've had a few problems with some of those people. This could be serious. I'll fly by the Big Island and pick up dad. He'll want to be in on this one," Cody said.

"Good. And tell Gary that Adi is a mess; he should call her from the air," Young Deer replied.

"Will do. Have your gear ready. We'll be there before you know it," Cody said and hung up the phone.

Young Deer walked around the desk and looked out at the marina.

"Billy, you've got yourself into a big one this time," he said aloud. He then dialed on the phone console on his mahogany desk.

"This is Bill. Get all of my diving and tropical survival gear together and deliver it to the dock. Take two M-16s with five clips each out of the armory, and throw in my Benelli 12 gauge and two boxes of shells. Tell Frank to gas up the cigarette boat and load two extra fuel tanks. I'm leaving in four hours. We'll need to get to Karkar Island pretty fast. Thanks," he said and hung up the phone.

Jon Nickerson jabbed Jack in the ribs with a Heckler & Koch G36 assault rifle to wake him up. This immediately woke up Randy since they were duct-taped back-to-back and jammed into a small closet off the main access tunnel to the rainforest. Nickerson took a knife from a scabbard on his belt and cut the tape. Jack looked up at the barrel of his rifle and recognized it from the spare thirty-round magazine attached to the side of the rifle. He had noticed it while observing British Special Forces in Africa.

"Get up. It's time to move," Nickerson instructed.

They soon emerged from the long tunnel into the dim daylight of morning. Sheets of water fell from the sky on the rainforest creating a surreal scene that would make for an expensive painting.

The sudden temperature change from the heated tunnel leading from the bowels of the volcano was a relief for everyone. Two armed men with Nickerson carried similar rifles and guarded Randy Heath and Jack MacGregor. The group emerged into a small clearing that held several metal buildings and an empty heliport. Randy and Jack were led into the first building, which appeared to be a repair garage for mining equipment and trucks.

"Over there," Nickerson ordered as the guards pushed Jack and Randy into a corner and ordered them to sit down. "Tie them up. I'll be back."

The two armed men then tied ropes around their wrists and ankles and walked across the garage to a refrigerator where they retrieved bottles of water. Nickerson walked into a small office at the end of the garage, closed the door, and turned on a radio. After a few minutes of adjusting dials and flipping switches, a voice on the other end could be heard.

"That's right, the snooping marine biologist came back, and this time he brought his buddy," Nickerson said. "He showed up just after you flew out of here."

"Are there others?" Akira Yoshida asked.

"No, just the two of them," Nickerson replied. "But I want you to send more men to hold this place together. Our workers surfaced, hijacked the three transports, and evacuated the mine. The quakes were a little too much for them, and I couldn't kill them all," Nickerson informed. "We were making good progress on the new vein."

"I can send you men from the Chungrebu mine where I just landed. They can intercept the transports and bring them back. There's only one road out of there. That should take about three hours or less. When they get there, get the workers down in the cavern next to the main vein and dig out as much as you can over the next twenty-four hours. Our estimates are that you can recover about twenty-five million dollars in gold nuggets from that one vein. Work them until they drop. If a worker refuses, kill him on the spot and push someone else to the front. Our profits are enormous. We can't afford to lose it now," Yoshida commanded.

"I agree. I'll take care of it," Nickerson replied.

"Stay until you finish one twenty-four-hour shift or the volcano begins to destabilize, then get out of there. Get rid of everyone. I don't want anyone left to talk about this vein, understand? We might be able to come back some day," Yoshida excitedly yelled.

"I understand completely."

"Signal us and I'll send a helicopter to pick you up. Send in the two scientists to dig and eliminate them with the workers," Yoshida directed and signed off.

Nickerson left the office and walked into the garage; he opened the refrigerator and quickly downed two bottles of cold water. He picked one up and walked over to Jack and Randy. He screwed off the lid and poured the cold water over their heads.

"I know, it's not the same as drinking it, but you got plenty of water down you while we were walking," he laughed.

"You're making a big mistake," Jack said.

"I am? I suppose you have a platoon of American marines out there who are coming to rescue you," Nickerson mocked.

"You could say that," Randy interjected.

"Well, if I were the two of you, I would enjoy my last minutes of life and think about where you've been and where you might be going. The natives call the cave the Devil's Breath. Could be it's as hot as that volcano out there, so enjoy this cool bit of heaven while you can," Nickerson scoffed and walked away.

The sun had risen but the monsoons allowed only a dull gray sky to reign over the rainforests of Papua New Guinea and the surrounding islands.

"I think we should move back to the beach," Mavis suggested and stood up.

"We can't leave Dad and everybody now," Heather countered.

"We can't help them either. If this volcano begins to blow, we're sitting in a very bad spot," Mavis said.

"Didn't Billy say that the spot where it would blow is at least ten miles away?" Heather argued.

"Yes, he did," R.O. agreed. "But these babies can shoot out boulders for miles that would crush you in a second. Hey, where'd Billy go?" R.O. asked, just noticing that he was gone.

"He woke me up and told me he was going back in to help Chris and Natalie. That's all the more reason to move away to a safe area. If we're here and they come back on the run, we'll just slow them down," Mavis reasoned.

"O.K. Let's go," Heather relented and stepped into the rain and walked toward the forest path that had brought them there.

Mavis and R.O. followed, disappearing behind some broad-leafed foliage.

The Falcon 7X touched down at the landing strip on Cape Gloucester. Young Deer was sitting in a Mercedes SUV waiting to pick up Cody and Gary Bridwell and take them immediately to the marina. Once inside the Mercedes and headed for the resort, the questions began to fly.

"Well, that sounds like something Billy would do," Gary, William Pfleiderer's World War II wingman, said. "We're just getting too old for these escapades, the last of a dying breed."

"I'll remember that Dad, when you go off on your next adventure. I suppose you want me to remind everyone that you entered the army at sixteen so they can do the math and say, 'Gee Gary, you look great for . . . '"

"Hold it there, son," Gary interrupted, and they laughed.

"On a more serious note, we've got torrential rains and rough seas. My new cigarette speedboat can handle just about anything. I noticed on the global radar that we have a break from heavy rains, just light and sporadic showers for the next three hours. We can quickly get to Karkar on the *Gloucester Rocket,* as I like to call her, in that time," Young Deer said and came to a stop at the marina.

Two resort employees walked over, grabbed four large plastic cases and put them on the boat while Cody, Gary, and Bill followed behind in the light showers passing overhead. Within minutes, the *Gloucester Rocket* was at sea and storming easily across the choppy seas at forty miles per hour with the help of her Caterpillar 660-horsepower motor. With a top speed of sixty in smooth water, they could easily reach Karkar Island in less than four hours. Each man put on a special upper body harness to stabilize their spines and prevent injury as the speeding boat jumped across the waves at high speeds.

After being gone less than two hours, the radio beeped and Young Deer triggered it for his headset.

"Bill here," he said.

"Bill, this is Adi. We finally got a satellite reading on Billy's boat. Don't know why it had not been picked up yet, but it's working now. That means they're in trouble. Let me give you the coordinates," she said.

As she read them out, Bill wrote them down on a small white board with a grease pencil that was attached next to the wheel.

"Got it. I'll give them to Cody, too. Take it easy, we'll find them all," Bill assured and clicked off the radiophone.

"Yea, I see that," Cody said as he leaned over to Bill to talk over the noise of the wind and motors. The half-canopy on the *Gloucester Rocket* only kept them partially dry. Gary had already retreated to the spacious cabin below.

Cody took out his waterproof satellite telephone and punched in a series of numbers. He waited about thirty seconds.

"G'day mate," greeted the Aussie voice on the other end.

"Steve, I've got new coordinates for you. Here they are." Cody read them off.

"Thanks boss. I've got six mates with me, and we're in the CH-47 Chinook with a heavy payload. Freddy's going to drop us at these new coordinates. Just a second . . . the computer just told me they're on the northeast beach of New Guinea across from Karkar Island. I'll meet you there in two hours," Steve Kash said.

"Good job, Steve. See you soon," Cody stated and ended the call.

"Sounds like all is set for the hunt," Bill said.

"We're prepared for whatever we find good or bad. These are the toughest Aussies I could get my hands on. Ex-special forces, you know the lot," Cody added and went below to put on his commando gear.

When he reappeared, he took the wheel from Bill.

"I know your size, big guy, and brought you a set too. Dad will help you with all the gear. When we hit the beach, he'll stay with the *Rocket,* and you can come along for the fun," Cody said with a serious look on his face.

"Well, I have to say it'll be more interesting than staffing or menu questions for sure," Young Deer replied.

"Any time you want to trade, you let me know," Cody smiled. "I would love to take over a resort. My kind of life will age you fast."

The time passed quickly, and soon the *Gloucester Rocket* was pulling up along side a radio antennae sticking out of the water. It was the burial spot of the *Desert Sailor.*

16

L.G.

"Haven't we been going too slow?" Natalie whispered to Chris in the long tunnel.

"No. We don't want to walk into something we're not prepared for," Chris replied.

"Isn't that a little too late?"

Chris turned around and gave her a stern look.

"O.K., it's not too late."

"You two quit talking. I can smell fresh air so we're getting close to the end of the tunnel," Billy ordered.

"I hope so. We've been down here for hours. I bet we've walked two miles," Natalie whispered.

This time Billy turned around and gave her a stern look.

"OK, OK. I'll be quiet. Maybe not that far."

"We had to take it slow. If we walked into the people holding Dad and Randy, we'd all be in bad shape," Chris said softly. "There's light just ahead."

"Let's keep it quiet and careful," Billy suggested and readied his weapon.

For an older man, Billy was in great shape and his warrior skills had not left him.

Chris and Natalie followed him closely until the end of the tunnel was in view. The closer they got, the louder the noise of the terrible weather outside.

"I smell the rain again. The sulfur was getting to me," Natalie complained. She held the pistol firm in her right hand, pointing it toward the ground.

"I'm going ahead to take a peek. Y'all wait here," Chris directed and walked by them carefully.

As he neared the opening, he crouched down low every few feet and listened. After confirming that no one was present, he went back to get Billy and Natalie. As they walked toward the large opening, they could see a road that entered the rainforest about one hundred yards away. Nothing else was in the area.

"This is strange," Billy observed. "No out buildings of any kind for communications, equipment repairs, or warehousing. Seems odd."

"Maybe they're in the forest," Natalie answered.

"I agree. They're probably being hidden by the foliage so they would be undetectable by air," Chris said.

"You're probably right," Billy agreed as a sheet of rain slapped into their faces.

"That felt great," Natalie said as she wiped the water from her mouth.

Suddenly there was a rumble down the tunnel, and the earth shook under their feet. Rocks and boulders began to roll off the mountainside down into the rainforest all around them. After about thirty seconds, it stopped.

"That was a big one," Billy said. "I think she'll blow pretty soon. We've got to keep moving."

"What about Mom, Heather, and R.O.?" Chris asked worriedly.

"They're supposed to head back to the beach. The little guys in the forest will probably intercept them after twenty minutes. Remember, that's their backyard out there," Billy replied.

The three felt another rumble deep in the earth and heard a loud explosion high on the mountain. Trees began to shake all around them. Birds took to the air as nature received her final warning.

"That was it," Billy announced and looked up in the sky expecting to see something through the rain but to no avail. "We've got to hurry now. It won't be long. Maybe on the next rumble she'll blow."

Two large multitrack trucks roared to a stop next to the metal garage; twenty heavily armed men clambered out and made their way inside out of the rain.

"Man are we in trouble," Randy Heath said and looked at Jack.

"I would have to agree," Jack replied.

"Where's Nickerson?" the leader of the group yelled at the two men sitting next to the refrigerator. He spoke with a strong German accent. Nickerson walked out of the office.

"It's about time you got here, Mueller," Nickerson said.

"We were sent to intercept the workers and restore order in the mine. I've got two dozen armed men. We caught most of the workers who jacked your trucks, but we heard the volcano start to go off just minutes ago; now there's not one man in my group willing to go into the mine," the big man with the German accent said.

"I understand. I heard it too, and I think it's getting too unstable. Just to let you know, I will promise fifty thousand dollars to every man willing to work for one hour on that vein of gold. If you work two hours, you get one hundred thousand dollars. You and I both know that this volcano may never blow. It's been here for centuries just rumbling and spewing; it may be another ten centuries before it blows it's cap. So what's your decision?" Nickerson asked, keeping his right hand on his holstered Beretta 9mm pistol.

"I'll do it," a man in the rear of the group said. "I'm pretty much a slave to this business even if I don't, so what's the difference?"

"I will too," another guard added until the whole band of men had agreed to go deep into the mine and work on the gold vein that was holding the large high-quality nuggets.

"Good. Go get your workers and get below fast," Nickerson demanded.

Just as Billy, Chris, and Natalie exited the mouth of the tunnel, they could hear the trucks rumbling up the road.

"Run into the forest," Billy ordered. He started walking as fast as he could in the heavy rain on the uneven turf and thought to himself, if this were water, he could make better time.

Chris grabbed him under one arm and Natalie under the other, and they began to run. Just as they reached the tree line, the first of the two trucks burst into the clearing. Men with guns pulled off workers from the trucks and escorted them at gunpoint back into the mine.

"They will all be killed," Natalie whispered quietly.

Chris put his right index finger to his lips and looked at Natalie.

All of the men had disappeared underground before the earth rumbled again. Then Billy, Chris, and Natalie heard the noise of a small ATV approaching the clearing.

"Dad," Chris said. Billy swiftly rotated and moved a few inches from his face.

"Shh," Billy said.

"That's Dad and Randy in the back," Chris whispered as the ATV disappeared into the tunnel leading into the bowels of the mine.

"Oh my gosh," Natalie said as tears escaped her eyes.

"This isn't good," Billy replied.

"What do we do now?" Chris asked.

"I don't know," Billy stated and shook his head. "I don't know."

"If I fall one more time, I'm not getting up," Heather declared as she straightened up from the mud, her blonde hair now brown and plastered against her head.

"Come on sweetie, I bet we're nearly there," Mavis encouraged and reached down for her.

"Mom, L.G. is back," R.O. said and turned toward his mother.

"L.G.? Ryan you make me so mad sometimes when you start fantasizing about things. I'm just too tired right now to get mad. Who is it you are talking about?" Mavis asked.

"The little guy with the little head around his neck. I call him L.G., just like R.O.," R.O. responded.

Mavis turned and found the short native islander blending into the rainforest rather easily.

"I see him too," Mavis acknowledged. "Oh, hello. Can you lead us to the beach, please?" Mavis asked, smiling as much as she could, wet to the skin, buried deep in the muck of the trail, and speaking as if quizzing a London bobby for directions at Trafalgar Square.

"Follow me," the tribesman said and started to walk away.

"Go slow, we're not moving too fast," Mavis requested.

The native islander looked back and stopped. Then he began again as they caught up. At this rate, Mavis thought, they might get back to the beach in two to three hours.

Young Deer circled the *Gloucester Rocket* around the antennae of the *Desert Sailor* for a few minutes while Cody made contact with his search team.

"You're how far from the beach? You're breaking up," Cody said.

"We should be there in ten to fifteen minutes. The rain's

picked up, and we've reduced our air speed quite a bit," Steve Kash, Cody's head of operations, said into the satellite telephone.

"We'll see you on the beach, mate," Cody replied to the Aussie from Perth.

"To the beach we go," Young Deer said and pushed the throttle forward on the giant speedboat.

In a few minutes, they were cruising alongside the beach looking for the spot where Billy and his crew had swum ashore.

"I've got it. There's a stack of palms on the beach lying in an unnatural position," Gary said. "I'll take the boat as close as possible; then you both can take the raft to shore."

Young Deer and Cody pulled a cord on the inflatable raft and tossed it over the side. After both were in, Gary flung over two duffel bags full of weapons and supplies. Just as they paddled up to the low rising surf of the tropical island, the whipping and chopping sound of a Chinook helicopter could be heard overhead. In next to no time, it was hovering five feet over the ocean about fifty feet from the beach. A rear platform opened, and a large crate fell out to the ocean. Three men, dressed in wet suits, jumped in behind them and connected a cable from the Chinook to the big crate. The large helicopter gently pulled the crate to the beach until it wedged in the sand. The two cables were disconnected, and Kash spoke to the pilot of the helicopter on his radio. After that, the pilot of the Chinook saluted Kash and Cody before turning the aircraft around and heading for a secure inland clearing to wait for further instructions. Young Deer, Cody Bridwell, and three commandos were now on the beach in Papua New Guinea.

As the men exited the water, Cody greeted each one personally. One of them pulled large pins on the side of the big crate; the front panel fell down on the wet sand with a thud. More rain began to fall as the men worked to free the machine inside. Young Deer stood and watched their efficiency until he heard a whirring noise coming from the crate. Suddenly a hovercraft emerged, sped higher on the beach, and settled down. The two other commandos quickly climbed aboard.

"Very efficient," Young Deer said as Cody walked up.

"Like our business motto says, *We provide more than security, we provide peace of mind*," Cody replied.

"No wonder profits have been up in that company," Young Deer added. "Keep it going. Now let's go find Billy."

"We've got to go back inside," Chris demanded.

"That would be too dangerous," Natalie responded as they watched a second group of armed men go into the tunnel with forced laborers.

"Dad and Randy have no hope of survival without our help," Chris replied. He wiped water from his face. The rain had soaked them to the skin again, and each could feel it in their socks and shorts.

"You think so?" asked Billy.

"You must go," Natalie said and began to tear up. She put her hand to her mouth and started to cry. "You have to go help them, Chris. Please don't die," she whimpered.

He turned to her and put his hands on her cheeks, brushed away her wet auburn hair from her forehead, and looked into her blue eyes.

"I wouldn't think of doing that. Relax," he said. He hugged her tightly. Afterward he picked up the M-16 and left the two in the forest. Running quickly to the tunnel opening, he stood next to it and peered deep inside. Then he turned to his right and disappeared.

"We need to move deeper into the forest," Billy said to Natalie as she wiped the tears away.

"You're right. Let's go." Natalie agreed.

Another rumble across the earth startled Mavis, Heather, and R.O. as a small earthquake shook the floor of the rainforest.

"Hey L.G.," R.O. said to the small native islander.

The short but stocky man with the human head dangling around his neck stopped and turned to R.O. and Mavis.

"My name Matthew," he said. "The name missionaries gave me. I like that one. But I like L.G., too. What does it mean?"

"It means Little Guy with the little head," R.O. replied with a smile.

"Little Guy with little head. O.K. Matthew can be L.G., too. We halfway there so need to rest. Where are other people?"

"They're still in the mountain," Heather answered as she leaned against a tree.

"They will be in danger when mountain wakes up."

"We had to leave and get out of the way," Mavis said, doubting her own statement and looking down at the leaf clutter on the forest floor.

"Mom, it's all right. Chris and Billy will find them. We would have just been in the way. Chris will know what to do," Heather stated confidently, trying to make her mother feel better.

As they talked, they began to hear a crashing noise echoing through the forest. With the rain continuing to fall, Mavis squeezed the water out of her hair. She had long before abandoned wiping it from her face. However, the crashing noise seemed to grow louder. She felt more rain flow down the back of her shirt, and with each blink of her eyelids, large water drops clung to her eyelashes.

"Mom, it's coming from over there," Heather said and pointed.

"Hide, please," Matthew warned and rushed into some tall bushes off the trail, disappearing quickly.

As it got nearer, the crashing noise turned into a whirring sound. Unexpectedly several trees were pushed to the ground when a camouflage-painted hovercraft passed about seventy-five feet from them.

"Steve, I'm getting a thermal reading of people or large mammals twenty meters to portside," Cody reported.

"Copy that," Kash replied.

"Who are those guys?" Heather asked as the hovercraft appeared through the dense foliage. "Look, that's Young Deer from the resort!"

Mavis stood and yelled, "Hello! Help!"

The Aussie sitting next to Kash swung around and pointed an automatic rifle at Mavis when she stepped out of the foliage. Her soiled bright pink tank top stood out from the greens and browns of nature.

"Friendly!" Young Deer yelled.

The Aussie lowered the rifle, and Kash brought the hovercraft to a halt. Mavis ran toward the craft.

"I'm Mavis MacGregor, and my husband and Dr. Heath have been taken captive," she screamed. "I think we've been wandering out in this forest for hours."

Young Deer hopped over the side of the craft and landed on the forest floor. He hurried over to Mavis.

"Remember me, Bill from the resort on New Britain," he said.

"Yes, Heather spotted you, thank goodness," she said. "We're so tired," Mavis continued. "If it weren't for the forest natives, we wouldn't have survived. The men who run this illegal mine in a large cavern of the mountain took Jack and Randy captive."

Cody walked up to her dressed in commando clothing, with a utility belt complete with a GLOCK M-27 .40 caliber pistol that could withstand water and a host of other problems and still fire. Extending his hand toward Mavis, he said, "My dad is Billy Fly's other partner. I'm Cody Bridwell, and these men work for me."

Without hesitation, she stepped forward and hugged him.

"I'm so glad you're here," she said.

"I like your hovercraft. Maybe I can go for a ride?" R.O. asked.

"Sure, but now I want everyone to go to the beach; we'll move forward and extract your husband and Dr. Heath," Cody ordered.

"My oldest son, Billy Fly, and Natalie are out there somewhere too," Mavis informed frantically.

Another large explosion was heard high overhead on the mountain. Little pellets of rock hit the leaves around them.

"Ouch," Heather yelled as a pellet-sized rock landed on her shoulder.

"Change of plans. Everyone on board," Cody shouted.

Mavis pushed R.O. over the side. Heather hopped on as if jumping over a fence. Young Deer reached out and grabbed Mavis by the arms, pulling her up and over the thick-walled sides of the hovercraft. L.G. disappeared into the rainforest.

"Head for the beach," Cody ordered.

"Wait! My son, Jack, Natalie, Mr. Fly . . . they're all still in the mine," Mavis shouted over the noise of the craft.

"We'll get you and the kids safely to the beach, and then we'll come back for them," Cody said quickly and firmly.

Mavis sat down and held on tight as the hovercraft turned and whirred back toward the beach, moving down the same trail from which they had just come. The assault craft traveled the distance in only twenty minutes compared to the two hours on foot. Once they made it to the beach, they radioed Gary, and he drove the *Gloucester Rocket* close to the beach. One of the Aussies fitted Mavis, Heather, and R.O. with life jackets as the hovercraft raced out to the cigarette boat. As Mavis stepped over the gunwale she looked back toward the rain-shrouded island and heard the volcano begin to rumble deeply within. Chills ran down her neck to her arms reaching her fingertips. Tears welled up in her eyes.

"Oh Jack, what have we done now?" she whispered.

17

Rivers of Fire

Chris MacGregor crept slowly down the tunnel that he, Billy Fly, and Natalie had left a few minutes earlier. He could hear the voices and machine noises of the men who were ahead of him. With the mining company shirt on, he thought he could blend in, or least he hoped he could.

As he approached the metal doors, which sealed off the mine, he waited for someone to come out so he could slip inside. There were no handles on his side, and he realized that it must open by radio. He leaned up against the moist rock and could feel the small tremors of the mountain trying to shake loose millions of tons of rock, thousands of cubic feet of carbon dioxide and sulfuric gas, and a host of other pollutants. Without warning, two armed men burst through the metal doors and disappeared into a side tunnel, interrupting his thoughts.

Chris sprinted toward the slowly closing door, just reaching it five inches from the jam. He caught it with his left hand and looked around. No one had seen him. He pulled the door open and glanced inside. He saw only one armed guard posted with his back to him. Chris raised the rifle butt high in the air and brought it down quickly on the man's neck. He fell limp to the ground.

"Sorry, buddy, but it's you or my dad, and I choose my dad," Chris said as he took the man's Taurus 9mm pistol and put it under his belt. He retrieved the guard's AK-47, pulled its magazine, and then ejected the round from the firing chamber. He was tossing the magazine into the darkness of the tunnel when he heard more machinery being turned on ahead in the cave.

Chris promptly moved forward until he was a hundred yards into the mountain. The heat had risen to over one hundred degrees and climbing. He finally reached the quarters and rooms where they had earlier found clothes, food, and water. There was no one in the canteen area so he walked into it as if he worked there. He had reached the large cooler and was drinking a bottle of water when two men walked in.

Startled by seeing a stranger there in a uniform shirt with a rifle slung over his shoulder, the men immediately trained their weapons on Chris. One of the men fired a round his way, and Chris jumped. As he fell behind a table, he fired off two rounds toward the guards who quickly disappeared from the room.

Right afterward a loud thud vibrated through the mine, and the mountain shook again. Without delay, Chris left the canteen. Finally reaching the main part of the mine, he crouched behind a four-foot high stack of drill bits. Although the teeth had been worn off, its steel composition would protect him if bullets started flying. Then he spotted his dad and Randy. They were bound together back-to-back with a rope and lying on the floor of the mine.

Several workers were lined up nearby with five guards pointing weapons at them. After a muffled pop, a new worker was led into the tunnel. Chris watched workers enter for fifteen minutes. Five more pops occurred, and no one came out. He was becoming nauseous by the killers' depravity; he feared for his dad's life.

"Silencer maybe. They're working them till they drop from heat and then killing them," he thought to himself. Sweating profusely, he could feel his heart beating faster in his chest.

At that point, a large crash sounded through the cavern, followed by the earth shaking all around him. A few large boulders fell from the ceiling of the mining cave and bounced like basketballs on the solid rock floor.

Remembering the cave in China, Chris uttered, "Not again."

Another large crash followed and more boulders loosened in the mammoth cave. Chris didn't know what to do. He realized that he would have to kill the guards to save his dad and Randy. It was a heavy decision for an eighteen-year-old boy, but he knew he had to do it. He had to save his father.

He went through the scenario in his mind. First, shoot each guard quickly, starting with the one closest to the tunnel opening. Next move down the line and kill anyone that steps toward the opening of the tunnel leading to the gold deposit. He had shot big game from farther distances but had not fired an M-16. He knew the high velocity of the round would help his aim, but he had to calm down immediately and breathe steady. He decided he would pull the trigger when the mountain stopped shaking. But the shaking didn't stop. It kept going and going and going. Another loud boom echoed through the cavern, and a large crack in the cavern floor opened about seventy-five feet from where Jack and Randy were lying.

Molten magma began to spew as the crack grew into a crevasse. The lava began to flow across the floor toward Jack and Randy. The five guards stepped back, and the workers began to run; Chris had his chance. One of the guards was able to shoot two workers before Chris could raise the M-16 and shoot him dead to stop the slaughter. He had no other choice; saving lives came first. Chris fired the weapon and ducked down. The guard dropped dead from the perfect shot. The other guards could not determine where the shot came from, so they retreated toward the barracks down the cavern. The remaining workers ran for the tunnel exit.

Opening fire and dragging bags of gold behind him, Jon Nickerson burst from the small tunnel. He fired his automatic rifle wildly toward Chris not knowing how many were assaulting the tunnel. Chris dove to the floor of the cave, rolling up against an excavating machine. Due to the ricocheting bullets, he kept his head down. One nicked his right shoulder causing a flow of blood to stream across is chest.

By then, Nickerson had disappeared up the entrance by the barracks. Chris looked up; everyone was gone except his dad and Randy. The lava was still running across the floor of the cave when a large crack in the wall next to Chris opened and lava poured from it. The searing hot fire from the new fissure raced down the wall and out across the floor consuming everything in its path. The temperature in the cavern reached 130 degrees Fahrenheit and continued to rise.

Chris stood up and ran for his father, sucking hard to breathe with each stride. As he reached Jack and Randy, he removed the utility knife from his belt scabbard. With a flip of his wrist, he opened it and began cutting the rope.

"Chris, where did you come from?" Jack asked as he pulled his hands and feet apart and picked up the AK-47 the dead guard had been carrying. Jack glanced at the guard and then at Chris. "Good shot, son. You did the right thing."

"Thanks," Randy said and got up. "You're a brave young man."

"This way," Chris directed and took off in a run. He heard the crack of a rifle from behind. Randy stumbled to the floor of the cave, and Jack spun and fired off six rounds. Jon Nickerson had stepped from the tunnel to take one last shot. He turned and disappeared. Making his way back to

Randy, Chris could see that he had been shot in the back of his left thigh.

"I can't walk. You guys go on," Randy pleaded.

"Not on your life, pal," Jack said. He pulled Randy up and guided his left arm around his own shoulders.

"Aghh," Randy screamed as the pain from his injured leg rushed through his body. "My leg may be broken."

"Doesn't matter, we're not leaving you," Jack replied. Three rounds whizzed by from the cave entrance as two more guards suddenly appeared.

Chris knelt and fired his entire clip; he heard two voices squeal in pain.

"Dad, give me your rifle, mine's empty," Chris called. "This 9mm won't be as accurate at this distance."

Jack handed him the AK-47. Chris opened the chamber to be sure a round was loaded, and it was.

Another loud rumble blasted through the cavern as the far wall opened, spilling more lava. Tongues of fire shot out across the floor and wall in the form of flowing lava. The temperature climbed to 140 degrees, and a crushing noise up the tunnel sent a plume of smoke and dust into the mining cavern. Chris fell to the floor, and the rifle bounced free from his grip and fell into a molten crevasse.

Chris, Jack, and Randy stopped, realizing their escape tunnel had just closed. They weren't the only ones. Armed guards appeared from the tunnel of gold, firing in all directions, fleeing for the exit tunnel. The three men took refuge behind a huge front-end loader. Bullets ricocheted off the large bucket on the front.

"I've got the Taurus 9mm and that's it," Chris said worriedly.

Jack tied off Randy's wound with his belt to slow the bleeding. Then another explosion roared through the cavern, and the wall behind them split open, spewing out fire and molten rock. The temperature in the cave seemed to jump another ten degrees in a matter of seconds.

When the guards realized their doom was imminent if they stayed where they were, the firing stopped. They made a rush for the worker's quarters and the exit tunnel, but realizing that passage was closed, they turned toward Chris, Jack, and Randy and the direction of the rock stairway one-third mile down the cavern that led to the top and out. Their assault began with a massive barrage of bullets!

On the return trip to the mine but still deep in the rainforest, Steve Kash was piloting the hovercraft with Cody, Young Deer, and another Aussie. The big but maneuverable machine ripped a path through the rainforest that would completely heal itself within a year. Suddenly they stopped because the craft closed to within ten feet of Billy Fly, who was waving his arms wildly.

"I knew you wanted to have the resort all to yourself but running me over in the rainforest never crossed my mind," Billy said.

"I'm too used to your old ways. Now get in, we're wasting time," Young Deer shouted over the noise.

"Don't forget about me," Natalie yelled as she ran from behind a tree.

The Aussies reached over to grab her outstretched arms and lifted her up and inside the hovercraft.

"Fasten that seatbelt and hang on tight," one of them said to her.

Billy Fly climbed up the rope ladder one of Cody's men had thrown over the side of the other craft. The hovercraft assaulted the thick rainforest by crushing everything in its path. Time passed swiftly, and they were now approaching the clearing next to the tunnel into the mine.

"That's where people and equipment enter the mine," Billy pointed out to Young Deer.

"Let's check the out building first. We may get lucky

and find them and get out of here quick," Cody said.

As the craft approached the buildings, Jon Nickerson, who had escaped from the mine, heard the loud machine and ran out the door. He saw the hovercraft, pulled out his pistol, and started firing. One of the Aussies was hit and fell out onto the road. Cody let out a barrage of bullets from his rifle. There was just enough delay that the bullets missed Nickerson but tore into the building itself. He rushed inside and then out the back door just as a gasoline tank inside the garage exploded. The whole building ignited into a ball of flames.

Another truck full of armed guards had just arrived from Chungrebu and opened fire from the edge of the rainforest. Heavily outgunned, Cody drove the hovercraft back into the rainforest as Kash jumped over the side and pulled his friend to the safety of the trees. Cody circled around to pick them up just as the volcano let out another burst of fire and lava, but it still had yet to lose its major dome in the crater above.

Chris fired the Taurus at the rushing guards. Their return fire sent sparks flying from bullets that hit the big machine shielding the three men.

"Chris, you've got to find the exit hole we came in and get out of here," Jack said.

"No, Dad, this is one time I'm not going to listen to you," Chris retorted as a bullet hit twelve inches from his face and ricocheted off the metal.

"O.K., then hear this. I've got Randy's wound tied off, but we can't stop the bleeding forever. He could lose his leg or die," Jack stated.

"I understand . . ." Chris was cut off in midsentence when part of the cavern roof over their head began to crack apart and fall. Jack and Chris pulled Randy under the big front-loader. Its tires were eight feet tall. Rocks and debris caved in around them. Then a stream of molten lava began to drip. When the lava hit one of the big tires, it exploded almost immediately with such a bang that Chris thought for a second he'd lost his hearing.

"Let's drag him. We've got no choice," Jack said.

Chris nodded in agreement, and they grabbed Randy under each arm and began to pull. Chris balanced the gun on Randy's shoulder and fired off two more rounds.

"That's my left ear you're messing with," Randy smiled. "But go ahead. Better deaf than dead."

Once they reached a stack of pipe, they stopped and looked back. The armed guards had stopped firing and had disappeared all together.

"Where'd they go?" Chris asked.

"I think they wanted to get away from this," Jack replied.

Chris turned around and said, "Oh, man."

"That's the biggest stream of lava I've ever seen up close," Randy said. His face was turning red from the heat.

The entire wall of the cave now seemed to be a river of lava about thirty feet wide; it consumed everything in its path. It blocked their way to the rock stairway, which led up and to the exit.

"I've got an idea," Chris announced. He let go of Randy's arm and took off in a run back toward the other end of the cavern.

"Chris," Jack called out but was ignored.

After running for a couple of minutes, Chris's heart was pounding in his chest. Running in the heat of the cave was like running against a strong wind coming from a blast oven. He slowed to a jog and finally reached the tractor-loader that Billy had used to knock down the brick wall. He had no energy left. He had to force every muscle to move to climb into the safe cage surrounding the driver's seat. He pushed on the ignition button, and the reliable Caterpillar fired up immediately. A huge grin crossed his face as he put it in gear and it began to move.

His face was swollen, and he had no more sweat to expel. His tongue felt as if it were three times its normal size. Flooring the accelerator, he drove it at high speed toward the opposite end of the cavern.

Soon Chris had reached the tunnel of gold and stopped. He left the motor idling as he hopped off and stepped over the bodies of two of the guards. He readied his pistol and entered the cave.

To his horror, he found a stack of bodies belonging to workers who couldn't maintain the production level Nickerson wanted. He reached down and picked up a large onion sack half full of gold nuggets. He then ran out of the cave and climbed back up to the driver's seat of the idling Caterpillar. Again accelerating, he quickly reached the spot where Jack and Randy were waiting. The heat was now climbing beyond the survival limits for humans.

"Chris, we're almost too exhausted to move. The heat will kill us in minutes if we don't get out of here," Jack yelled above the noise. "Randy is unconscious."

"I know, Dad. I've got a plan. Let's get him on the Caterpillar," Chris responded.

Jack and Chris lifted the near lifeless body of Dr. Randy Heath high onto the large machine and climbed up. Chris turned the giant machine around and drove the one hundred yards from the growing streams of fire running across the cavern.

"I get it," Jack said. "Let's do it!"

Chris began to accelerate the machine to its top speed. He knew the second he hit the fiery lava the tires would explode. But he was hoping that his speed would carry the big tractor across the streams of lava. Jack also knew that the machine might lurch from the heat and melt under them, which meant instant death. They had no choice. The heat and gases in the cavern would kill them in a few minutes anyway.

The big Caterpillar raced across the cavern floor and

made it to the fiery streams. All four tires exploded instantly, and the machine dropped three feet down into the lava
as the tires melted away. The momentum slowed, and they
came to a halt.

"Let's crawl out the front and jump off," Jack suggested,
pulling Randy's arm.

Chris pushed from behind as the big tractor began melt-
ing out from under them.

Pulling the limp marine biologist with all of his strength,
Jack shouted, "Faster."

When they reached the end, Jack jumped off onto dry
ground just inches from the flames. Chris pushed Randy
into Jack's arms, which made him fall backward to the
ground. Jack took Randy's arms and dragged him away
from the flow of lava.

Suddenly the tractor lurched to its side, and Chris
reached for anything he could find to keep from falling off
into the fiery stream.

"Chris!" Jack exclaimed.

Without answering, Chris crawled back to the motor
housing and looked out at the stream, which was now carrying the big tractor away from the dry ground. He
grabbed the sack of gold and threw it toward Jack and
Randy where it landed safely.

Touching the heated metal, Chris yelled, "Ouch." He
looked back and balanced himself enough to reach the driver's cage. Gauging the distance from the front of the tractor
to dry ground, he knew that if he missed, his feet and legs
would be incinerated before his body could feel the pain.
Then he would sink into the molten mass and burn to ashes
in seconds, fully aware of the pain and his upcoming death.

He took off in a run on the ten-foot motor casing of the
tractor and jumped with all of his might at its end. As he
flew through the air, his lungs filled with the hot gases rising from the fire below, which stung inside his chest. Like
a long jumper, he forced his legs out in front of him and

crunched into a ball. The solid ground under his feet jolted him and forced him to roll on the hard floor of the cavern. Pushing himself up, he felt something hot on his feet and noticed his shoes' heals were melted flat.

"Chris," Jack said and grabbed him.

Without saying another word, they dragged Randy over to the stairs. They stood him up, and Jack laid him across his back and started up. The arduous climb to the top took five minutes, with Chris balancing Jack from behind, pushing him all the way to the top. When they reached the small room leading outside, a cool breeze hit Chris in the face. With the sack of gold nuggets in his right hand, Chris turned and looked out across the expanse of the cavern. Fire and death were everywhere. He now understood why the natives called it the Cave of the Devil's Breath.

18

Ashes on Paradise

As Chris and Jack carried Dr. Randy Heath out of the rock corridor, a wall of water rushing off the mountain drenched them. Steam rose from their overheated skin. Chris and Jack sighed and collapsed to their knees, letting the rain rinse off the dirt and heat of the mine. They leaned Randy up against the wall of the mountain and washed his face. The heat dissipated with the fresh water, and his face began to regain its normal color.

Jack picked up a large leaf that had trapped water from the falling rain, and he funneled the liquid into Randy's mouth. Once his body temperature dropped, Randy began to wake. His leg was not broken, but the wound still dripped blood despite the tourniquet Jack had tied securely around it, which he was now opening for a minute to let blood flow to Randy's foot. Then they heard gunfire about a hundred yards away.

"Sounds like a war," Chris observed.

"It probably is. I'm going to go help, you stay with Randy," Jack said.

"Thanks, Dad, but you need to stay with Randy. You

know more about how to help him than I do," Chris replied
and handed Jack the bag of gold.

"What's this?" Jack asked.

"We'll talk about it later," Chris answered and ran
toward the gunfire.

Jack stood Randy up and helped him over to the edge of
the forest to hide. Chris hurried along the best he could
after the heat had sapped his energy. As he approached
the firefight, he crouched down and readied the Taurus
9mm, not knowing how many rounds remained in the
clip. He could hear men yelling orders and a loud
mechanical whirring noise. Then the ground around his
feet began to shake, and with an enormous roar, the volcano blew its top!

Rocks and small boulders began to fall everywhere. Kash
reversed the hovercraft and maneuvered into the rainforest. He didn't know that Nickerson had radioed for an
escape chopper, a plan he had devised for such an event.
He had stashed a Kawasaki KLX 450 in a tool shed and had
already escaped through a jungle trail into the mountains,
with two saddlebags full of gold nuggets, headed for a rendezvous point. Now, Nickerson was the least of their worries as nature had unleashed a storm the likes they never
had seen.

Chris fell to the ground and saw the hovercraft with Billy
Fly and Natalie in the back. He got back up and waved his
arms frantically. Cody saw him.

"Look, that must be the MacGregor kid. Head that way,"
he announced.

"That's Chris," Natalie yelled over the noise.

Kash turned the craft around and darted across the clearing, constantly being pelted with small rocks and chips the
size of fine gravel. It was a surreal scene of heavy rain
mixed with fiery rocks and the beginning of an ash storm.

Young Deer turned and pointed across the clearing
toward the road.

"Would you look at that," he said quickly.

"A Sikorsky helicopter has landed. Looks like two men are hauling bags of something from that shed," Billy noticed. "They're hauling out the gold!"

Young Deer took over the throttle from Kash, who dug out helmets from the side storage and passed them to the passengers. Young Deer pushed the throttle forward, and the craft sped through the opening with flaming rocks bouncing all around them.

"Dad and Randy are under the ledge," Chris shouted as they drove up and stopped.

"Hop in," Billy said.

Chris jumped over the side and pointed toward where Jack and Randy were hiding. Within seconds, the hovercraft was sitting still next to Jack.

Young Deer jumped out, picked up Randy, and pushed him high on the side of the craft. Billy and Natalie pulled him the rest of the way.

"We've got to get him back to the beach and away from all of this," Cody informed.

"Gotta go, Dad," Chris stated quickly.

"Wait," Jack replied.

"I'm not letting that chopper take off," Chris answered.

"I agree. Let's go," Jack responded.

"Here!" Young Deer shouted and tossed a M-16 rifle down to him.

"Thanks," Jack yelled and started out in a run behind Chris.

Small rocks and flaming boulders bounced all around them. Jack fired a round over the heads of the men loading the helicopter, and they ducked to the ground. Chris and Jack reached the Sikorsky just as it was powering to take off, and Jack stood in front of the pilot, aiming the rifle through the glass window. The pilot raised his hands, and the men in the back jumped out and ran into the rainforest.

Opening the pilot's door, Chris ordered, "Get out."

The pilot got out and moved away from the helicopter. Out of nowhere, a ten-pound rock hit him in the shoulder and knocked him to the ground.

"Let's get out of here, Dad," Chris cried out, jumping into the pilot's seat and strapping in.

Jack ran around and hopped up through the copilot's door. Chris pulled on the collective and the cyclic, and the chopper began to lift off. He pulled up hard and fast and soon was high in the clouds, the mist of the rainforest, and the erupting volcano. Ash on the windshield was mixing with the rain making it a thin gray mud that Chris tried to clear with the wipers.

Turning hard over the trees and away from the angry mountain, he soon was free of the falling rocks that would damage the helicopters delicate fuselage and rotary blades. He flipped on the radar switch and quickly discovered that tall mountains surrounded them on three sides. His only avenue of escape was toward the ocean.

"We've got to go higher than this ridge," Chris said.

Abruptly the radio squawked and a familiar voice was heard.

"This is Nickerson, can you read me?"

"That's the guy from the cave," Jack commented.

"Answer him, but change your voice. Pretend he's hard to hear," Chris responded quickly.

"Can barely read you, Nickerson," Jack said. "Over."

"I'll be at the rendezvous in ten minutes. What's your twenty?" Nickerson asked.

"You're breaking up. We'll be there to meet you. Is that LZ 1 or 2?" Jack inquired.

"What the heck are you talking about? It's due east of the mine ten klicks," Nickerson shot back.

"Roger," Jack replied and turned off the transmission. "Can you get us there?" he asked to Chris.

"I'm already making the correction, but the ash cloud

will be very close. If we suck that up in the engine, it's all over for us," he replied.

Meanwhile the hovercraft was forging through the rain-forest on the less than an hour trek back to the beach. Kash, a former paramedic with the Royal Australian Navy Seals, was tending to Randy's injured leg.

"The bleeding's stopped. He'll be fine and keep the leg, too," he said.

"That's a relief," uttered a delirious Dr. Heath from his loss of blood.

"Good job," Billy acknowledged and sat back down as he ducked a low hanging branch. "Are we going back after Chris and Jack?"

"I don't think so. The volcano is only going to get nastier," Cody responded.

"What? We're not going back?" Natalie asked hysterically.

"We can't," Cody said. "You saw them take off. They could be anywhere."

"We just can't leave them there," Natalie stated again.

"Calm down, missy," Billy said. "I think your boyfriend and his dad can take care of themselves. They'll find a way to stay out of harm's way."

Natalie just sat back down and put her face in her hands.

Chris was maneuvering the Sikorsky through the clouds, stealing peeks of the rough terrain below, when suddenly he felt a thud on the side of the chopper.

"Must have been a pretty good size rock," Jack said.

"Lucky it didn't knick a prop or go right into the engine," Chris responded and pushed the helicopter closer to the jungle below.

"Have you seen any roads or trails yet?" he asked Jack.

"Not yet. It's really thick down there," Jack replied. "I'm impressed with your flying, son."

"I'd forgotten you've never flown with me before."

"Nope, wait. I see something moving. It's yellow, yes it's a motorcycle," Jack observed. "It must be a small trail, and he's heard us by now, I'm sure."

"Let's move ahead and find the clearing," suggested Chris.

Chris pushed the throttle forward to increase air speed, and it hadn't been two minutes before that a large clearing at the top of a ridge was spotted.

"Let's sit down and give Mr. Nickerson a surprise welcome," Jack said.

"Going down," Chris replied as he slowed and coasted to a soft landing.

"We've got about three or four minutes," Jack warned. He hopped out and ran toward some bushes at the edge of the clearing.

Chris began powering down the helicopter and climbed into the passenger compartment. He checked the pistol; it had two rounds in the clip and one in the chamber. He stepped across the bags full of gold nuggets and lay down flat on the seat. He then heard a dirt bike whining up the trail toward the clearing.

Another minute passed before Nickerson drove up to the helicopter, grabbed the saddlebags, and laid the motorcycle on its side. He looked around at the abandoned chopper and frowned. A roar behind him told him the volcano had sent another blast of lava, rock, and ash out of its dome. Nickerson reached up, pulled the handle to the side door, and swung it open.

"Greetings," Chris announced and pointed the gun at his face. "Hands high in the air."

"Don't do anything stupid," bellowed Jack as he ran up behind him. He reached under Nickerson's arm and pulled the Beretta 9 mm out of the holster and stepped back.

"Smarter than what I gave you credit for, are you?" Nickerson smiled.

"You just don't know who you are dealing with," Chris replied.

"Who, a smart-mouthed kid and his daddy?" Nickerson asked. "You better put down your guns. You're messing with the big leagues now."

"So the big leagues murder people because they can't dig fast enough?" Jack retorted.

"That's right. People are just tools. Whether it's digging for gold, diamonds, or anything of value, using people is just another means to accumulate wealth," Nickerson spat out.

"And power?" Jack added

"Right again. What is this? A quiz? There's enough gold in that helicopter to make you and your kid millionaires for life. Don't be stupid. Let's all fly out of here, head over to Port Moresby, and go our separate ways."

"Not even tempting. I saw how you killed those innocent men," Jack replied.

"Dad, we've got a problem. The wind's shifting," Chris informed him as he stepped down from the helicopter. "In a few minutes, we'll be covered with ash."

"O.K., Nickerson, get in the back and strap on a seatbelt," Jack ordered and poked him with the barrel of the rifle.

In a couple of minutes, Jack and Nickerson were in the back with Jack holding the rifle toward the Canadian mining engineer. As the wind began to blow the ash cloud right at them, Chris had already powered up the chopper and was lifting off.

"We've got to get moving," Chris said. He pulled hard on the controls and steered away from the cloud. "I'm heading northeast toward the ocean, Dad."

"OK, son. Get us out of here," Jack replied anxiously.

Jack never lost eye contact with Nickerson. The Sikorsky climbed, leaving the mountain ridge, and made a run for the ocean. However, the winds of the upper atmosphere pushed the volcanic cloud toward them faster and faster.

The hovercraft had just arrived on the beach when the last blast reverberated across the top of the rainforest.

"Wow, that was a big one," R.O. exclaimed as Billy and Natalie crawled down from the hovercraft.

Soon everyone was standing on the beach watching the lava flow down the side of the volcano.

"I don't know. That new flow is on our side of the mountain," Cody stated with a worried look on his face.

"You're right. My guess is that it could be here on the beach in less than an hour. Maybe two," Billy added.

"I better call the *Rocket*," Young Deer said.

Five minutes later, Gary Bridwell was bringing the cigarette speedboat as close as he could get to the beach. Within minutes, the hovercraft was tied alongside.

"Dad, the cloud is gaining on us," Chris said in a worried tone.

"Better look for a landing spot, son," Jack replied.

"Why don't you two just face it; you're not going to bring me in," Nickerson snickered with a smile.

Jack ignored the comment and continued to look at the cloud racing toward them.

"Here it comes," he shouted to Chris.

"Hold on," Chris yelled back.

Within seconds, all the warning lights began to flash and the buzzers began to screech through the cockpit as the engine seized and the rotary wing began to stop.

"Ready to auto rotate," Chris let out quickly, fighting the controls.

As the helicopter lost airspeed, it began to drop like a big rock. Only after five hundred feet did the big rotary wing begin to reverse itself and slow down the descent.

"We're headed into the trees," Chris revealed as the helicopter hit the first of the rainforest canopy's three tiers.

The noise of cracking glass, compressing metal, and breaking branches reverberated through their ears as the Sikorsky dove into the foliage of the rainforest as if it were an oceanic bird diving into a large blue ocean. The big helicopter bounced off the cushion of the third tier of the rainforest canopy like a child jumping on a trampoline. The massive rotors continued to spin, snapping limps and finally beginning to chip away.

The tail rotor suddenly snagged, sending the broken chopper cartwheeling end over end until there were no more trees, just the blue ocean below. Chris braced himself for the crash when he realized the grinding noise of the trees had ceased, meaning only one thing, they were free falling in air once again.

As the cracked windshield headed toward the sea, Chris instinctively put his arms across his face and closed his eyes. No thoughts rushed through his mind; he knew only that he needed to take a large breath of air as water rushed in around him. The helicopter doors ripped off, sinking instantly in thirty feet of warm water.

Chris frantically struggled with his seat belt and pulled himself free of the mangled front of the helicopter. He looked back into the compartment searching for his father, but the seawater burned his eyes and his lungs cried out for fresh air. Swimming to the surface, he took a breath of air and dove back down to the wreck sitting on the bottom of the lagoon. He searched the wreck but found no trace of his father. Satisfied that Jack was not in the water, he swam to the beach and dragged himself into the sand.

The volcanic cloud had turned and stayed inland; he was grateful for that. Rain continued to pour. With agony in his heart for his father, he struggled to his feet. He had begun walking toward the forest when he noticed someone bobbing in the ocean surf. He ran back into the water and recognized his dad trying to swim to shore.

"Dad. Dad!" he yelled as he bounded into the water and began pulling him to shore.

"Dad. Are you alright?" Chris asked anxiously.

"Yes. I just had the wind knocked out of me when I fell out over the water. Nickerson came out first over the trees. I never saw him again after that. Then before I knew it, we were in the ocean. Are you O.K.?" Jack asked.

"Yea, I'm fine. I was just worried about you," Chris replied.

"Look behind you," Jack instructed.

All of a sudden, there was a rustling noise in the bushes around them. Four native islanders, with brightly painted faces and shoulders, stepped forward. They all had white hair and shoulders from the falling volcanic ash. One of them had a shrunken human head dangling around his neck from a leather string.

"Where have you guys been? We've been waiting for you," Chris asked and smiled.

Epilogue

New Britain Island

Two of Billy Fly's employees pushed a cart carrying the heavy safe from the Japanese ship across the dining hall floor. It was after the morning rush and before lunch so no guests were present, except for the MacGregors and Natalie. The two men rolled the cart onto a sidewalk leading to the sandy ground around the mumu pit. They carefully lifted it off and set it upright on the sand.

Another employee walked in with a portable cutting torch; he knelt down beside the safe and looked up at Billy Fly, Adi, and Young Deer. Cody and Gary walked up just as the worker fired his torch. Dr. Randy Heath, on crutches, and his wife, Barbara, were following them. Gary and Cody balanced Randy on opposite sides when he stepped onto the sand around the pit to be closer to the safe.

"Ready . . . uh, bosses," the resort employee said and smiled.

Gwennie Zorger had also made an appearance for the occasion to represent the government's interest in the safe. She pulled up a chair next to Adi. Mavis was on her fourth cup of coffee and wired.

"Wait," Jack said. "I think Chris should have a chance to say something before the safe is opened. After all, he's the legal salvager of it."

"Illegal," Gwennie added and stroked Kitty Koo, who was purring in her arms and smelled of raw fish.

"Well, that's beside the point. He discovered it," Jack countered.

"No, Dad, I discovered it," R.O. boasted. "R.O. the treasure finder at it again."

"Makes no difference to me if it's the little guy or the big guy; somebody's got to be fined, and somebody goes to jail," Gwennie said and looked over the top of her glasses at a withering R.O., stepping behind Heather to block his mother's view.

At that moment, a tall sleek-looking brunette wearing tan summer linen pants and a matching jacket with a yellow silk blouse briskly walked toward the mumu pit followed by one of Billy Fly's security guards. A uniformed policeman walked behind them.

"Boss, I tried to stop her, but she's got the constable with her," the security guard said to Billy.

"That's alright. I'm Billy Fly, can I be of service to you?" he asked.

"Yes, Mr. Fly," she said with a French accent. "My name is Margo. I work for the International Committee for Historical Preservation in Geneva. I believe that the safe you are holding has documents of great importance."

"How would you know that?" Jack asked as he stood up. "I'm Dr. Jack . . ."

"I know who you are, Dr. MacGregor," Margo interrupted.

"Excuse me," Mavis stated with an angry look on her face.

"And you are also Dr. MacGregor," Margo replied. "And you are Chris MacGregor, the salvager of the safe and the one with whom I choose to speak."

"Listen, honey, you're going to have to speak to me, too," Gwennie spoke up.

"And who are you?" Margo smugly asked, flaunting her French accent.

"I'm Gwendolyn Zorger, regional chief inspector for the Department of Historical Preservation, Province of West New Britain, Independent State of Papua New Guinea. We own that safe regardless of who found it."

"We shall see," Margo said. "Shall we proceed with the opening of the safe?"

Billy Fly looked at his employee holding the cutting torch and nodded his head. The man leaned down and touched the flame to the top hinge of the safe; the hissing noise got louder until he had cut through the first hinge. Then he put the flame to the second hinge and quickly cut through the old metal. Turning off the torch, he retrieved a metal pry bar from his tool kit; he worked it into the seam and hit it hard with a hammer. It didn't budge. The door was tightly sealed. He struck it again and again; on the fourth strike it popped off and fell to the sand. He picked up his tools and moved back.

Chris stepped forward, bent down, and looked into the safe. He slowly reached in and pulled out a stack of Japanese paper money and laid it down. He next took out a small stack of photographs. Lastly, he pulled out a black leather folder embossed on the cover with gold Japanese characters.

Chris looked around at everyone and then walked back the few feet to the covered dining area. He sat down at a dining table and placed the leather folder on the white linen tablecloth. As Gwennie picked up the money and photos and put them in a shoulder bag, Margo walked over and sat down next to Chris. She produced a pair of archivist's cloth gloves from her handbag and put them on.

"May I?" she asked and picked up the old folder, setting it square in front of her.

Everyone in the room moved around and looked down at the strange faded black leather folder.

"The leather tie string is still intact. The safe must have been air tight for all of the papers to survive in the ocean that long," Margo said.

"I thought so. It was easy to maneuver off the ship and across the bottom of the lagoon," Chris commented softly.

Mavis just raised her eyebrows, looked at the ceiling, and let out a sigh.

"I knew we would be in trouble," Natalie said, sitting next to him.

Margo carefully untied the leather strings and laid them out across the table. Kitty Koo let out a big meow as Gwennie leaned across the table.

"Don't get any ideas about running out of here with the goods, lady," she spoke. "I can have you arrested too, you know."

"I won't be running anywhere, I assure you, Madam," was Margo's reply.

"And don't call me Madam, either," Gwennie barked back.

Margo carefully opened the front of the leather folder and pulled out a faded red leather-bound notebook roughly five inches by seven inches. On the cover, embossed in gold, were the words . . .

A.E.
The Around the World Flight Log
Lockheed Electra 10E
Purdue University

Presented by
Franklin Delano Roosevelt
President of the United States of America

"May I present to you the lost flight log of Amelia Earhart," Margo revealed.

"Oh, my gosh," Heather declared first.

"We're rich!" R.O. yelled out.

"Jack, do you know what this means?" Mavis asked. "Our son has made one of the greatest historical finds of the century."

"But how in the world did it end up in the safe of a captain of an Imperial Japanese Navy destroyer?" Billy Fly asked.

"It's a little bigger than our standard issue flight logs of the day," Gary informed. "Didn't she work for Purdue or something?"

"She did. She flew for them and taught aviation," Billy replied. "They even financed the Lockheed aircraft."

"Where did the A.E. come from?" R.O. asked.

"That's obvious, dodo head," Heather whispered.

"Heather," Mavis said sternly.

"She was known as A.E. among her friends," Margo said. "And President Roosevelt presented her with the specially made logbook in the White House before the flight. Conventional logbooks were smaller and didn't have the space she needed to record data about the flight."

"Well, let me ask it again. Why was it in the safe on that ship?" Billy repeated.

"That's what we, I mean my team, had just discovered when Chris salvaged the safe before we could get to it. He beat us by only a few hours, and we've been searching for seven years," Margo answered.

"Way to go, Chris," R.O. popped off again.

"Shut up, Ryan, and I mean it," Mavis fussed, sending arrows from her eyes to his.

"There have been many theories about how the world famous flyer disappeared," Margo began. "Some say she landed on Gardner Island and starved to death only to have her bones misidentified years later. Some say her plane simply ran out of fuel, and she crashed landed into the sea and perished. While others believe, she landed on an island occupied by the Imperial Japanese Navy, became an early

prisoner of a nondeclared war, and was executed for spy-
ing. No one knows for sure."

Margo turned through the pages of the logbook to the
final entry and began to read.

> July 2, 1937. Haven't been able to contact the Itasca for
> final approach to Howland Island. We must land soon and
> will look for anything that resembles a flat runway like a
> beach or coral atoll. Might have lost our antennae on take-
> off from Lae. We've just spotted an island that looks inhab-
> ited. We're taking her down.

"That's the last entry. Although I don't know which
island she landed on, this entry supports our theory that
she was indeed captured by the Imperial Japanese Navy
and held prisoner on Saipan. Of course, the Japanese could
have found her remains and the airplane in tact and kept
them from the U.S. because of the war. We know that
Yamamoto was privy to her capture, but we can't say he
was responsible for her death. There are too many loose
ends to blame the Japanese."

"Our researchers picked up a trail a few years ago
when studying maritime artifacts in Tokyo. We found a
list of personal belongings of Admiral Yamamoto that
were kept from his family after he was killed April 18,
1943, but instead of being returned to the family, they
were to be held by the admiral of the Imperial navy. One
of the entries, simply written in Japanese characters, stated "flight log." We assumed it was Yamamoto's flight log
or a diary of some sort. It didn't connect that he had never
been a pilot."

"However, our resident Japanese navy historian said
that Yamamoto's diary was delivered to his widow a
month after his death during his national funeral. Then
we went backward and followed all of Yamamoto's post-
ings leading up to the different myths about Yamamoto's
lost gold in the Philippines. It is on an inventory of his

headquarters in the Philippines that we find the "diary of the aviator" listed for the first time," she said.

"You knew it had to be a different officer, didn't you?" Billy Fly asked.

"Yes, we did. We had misinterpreted the original listing in Japanese. It was indeed listed as "flight log of the admiral" instead of "flight log belonging to the admiral." It was there all along. The Imperial Japanese Navy knew that he had it and was trying to find it after his death, subsequently adding it to the list of items to be returned to Tokyo to be hidden for all time. They didn't want anyone to know about it. Then we had to find where it had been taken. Yamamoto was transferred to Rabaul for the assault on the Allied Forces in the South Pacific but for some reason had called for his personal books and papers to be sent later. They were sent with a naval battle group that was headed south to beef up the Japanese after the loss at Guadalcanal," Margo informed.

"I remember that one," Gary said. "We won, but it was a tough battle!"

"Who's to say why he wanted all of his things and why they weren't flown in?" Margo stated.

"They weren't flown in because we ruled the skies," Billy Fly said.

"O.K., gentlemen. Let the nice lady talk. We don't need to relive every moment of the war," Adi interrupted.

"Well, the belongings appear on various lists of cargo taken aboard cruisers, aircraft carriers, battleships, and finally the destroyer *Arashio Maru*. I did some research on you two gentlemen," she said, looking at Gary and Billy Fly. "The *Arashio* belonged to the same battle group as the *Kako,* which you say you sank with your P-38s. The *Arashio* was sunk one month before Yamamoto was ambushed and killed by the Americans. We think that Yamamoto had given the flight log to the captain of the *Arashio,* one of his favorite officers."

"We only learned that when Yamamoto's family let us read his personal diary two years ago. Then we had to track down all of those officers of the Imperial navy who served under Yamamoto whom he might have favored. We soon developed a trail by connecting the dots across the South Pacific to find the most favored among his officers. However, we also discovered that most of them had died in battle at sea."

"We feared any evidence tying Amelia Earhart to the Japanese during World War II was on the bottom of the ocean already digested by a tubeworm or something," Margo said and stopped.

She looked around at everyone.

"The *Arashio Maru* was our last stop, but we couldn't find the captain's safe even after two salvage trips to the lagoon. We were headed back to a land site to get a blueprint of the ship that had been e-mailed to us when we spotted your airplane in the lagoon. We just knew we were late. When we dove back down and discovered the false wall that you had torn down, we knew that you had found the safe."

"Destroying historical artifacts is another offense and fine," Gwennie said, staring at Chris.

"Oh my," Natalie mumbled quietly.

"My feelings too," Mavis said to her.

"It fits with Yamamoto's character. He knew he couldn't win, but he also knew he couldn't let his young officers down either," Jack added.

The whole group fell silent.

"Amazing. Absolutely amazing," Gwennie spoke first. "The flight log will be the prize artifact at the new Center of History and Antiquities at Port Moresby."

"Wait. My team has been searching for the logbook for years. It will be returned to Geneva for the world to study and enjoy. We thought it was lost to all history," Margo said and stood up, pushing her beautiful brunette hair behind her right ear. "We search out the remotest of stories that history has given up on, and then we go after them. We find over half of what we search for," Margo said self-righteously.

"Perhaps the government of Papua New Guinea will be happy to work out a loan arrangement for a proper fee," Gwennie replied and petted Kitty Koo.

"We need to let these two ladies work this out. I think we should move over to the refreshments bar and have coffee and soft drinks," Billy Fly suggested.

"Good idea, Mr. Fly," Mavis said.

After everyone had moved to another table and fresh coffee, sodas, and pastries had been delivered, Jack stood up.

"I think Chris has something to share with all of us. Chris," he said.

"Well, I have been doing a lot of thinking since we took the safe; we didn't quite know what to do about it. We should have reported it right away. That would have been the right thing to do. But we didn't, and so it looked like we were trying to steal it. We weren't, but it looked that way. I'm glad that the contents won't belong to anyone in particular but will be shared with the whole world."

"And you get the credit," Natalie added and smiled. "Oops. I'll be quiet."

"Dad and I have all the gold we found in the first sack from the cave, and it comes to $143,080. Then we took the five sacks we found at the helicopter wreck site, and they come to $1.2 million. And Natalie had $9,000 in her pockets.

"Yup, I did. Big pockets," she said coyly and shrank back in her chair.

"Mr. Fly had even more in his pockets. So the total is, well you can do the math. Gwennie has already spoken to the Papua New Guinea authorities; they've agreed to use the money to build a clinic on the northeast coast near the tribe that helped us. They offered us a finder's fee of fifteen percent, or about $200,000," Chris stated.

"We're rich! What's my cut?" R.O. exclaimed.

"Nothing," Mavis answered quickly.

"Adi paid the insurance premium so I'll order another boat, *Desert Sailor II*," Billy said. "I don't need any of it. And my partners are writing off the rescue as a training event. Cody has already recovered the hovercraft from the beach and Dr. Heath's airplane, and I wanted to help the natives in the first place."

"So we've decided to pay for the rest of Natalie's college tuition from the finder's fee, invest part of it for college for our three, and use what's left to finance the rest of the adventures around the world," Jack said.

"Don't forget Randy," Mavis spoke quickly.

"We also shared some with Dr. Heath so he could become a partner in the Long Island Pearl Company and hire more local employees," Jack said.

"Thanks, Jack," Randy said and put his arm around his wife, Barbara.

"Good job, MacGregors," Gary said.

"I can't believe it," Natalie said as she hugged Mavis. "Thank you so much. Wait until my parents find out."

"And I almost forgot, we're also going to give ten percent of it to our favorite environmental fund," Jack said.

Gwennie and Margo, who had been listening to the conversation, walked up together.

"The Papua New Guinea gold mine environmental cleanup fund would be a great place to leave it," Gwennie said. "No one gets a fine, and no one goes to jail for taking the safe because you were so upfront about the gold. The government decided to treat the assets of an illegal mine just as we do illegal drug dealer assets. We're going to follow a paper trail and confiscate as much of the assets of this illegal company as possible, starting with the refinery at Karkar Island. Margo and I have also worked out where the new home of the Amelia Earhart flight log will be for now. It will go to Port Moresby, but we both agree that the politicians will probably fight it out as to where it may actually reside permanently. I'm sure that the Smithsonian and the

National Air and Space Museum will want it as well. Who knows? Maybe Amelia's home state of Kansas would want to exhibit it for a while."

Heather was the first to cheer, as everyone started clapping and hugging.

"No jail time, big boy," Natalie rejoiced as she hugged Chris and gave him a kiss.

He blushed.

"How's the leg, Randy?" Jack asked as Randy hobbled up beside him.

"It's great and Roosevelt called me to say the toxin levels have dropped. Looks like the pearl beds will be coming back."

"That's good news." Jack patted him on the back. "Nickerson's body was never found, and the native islanders think he probably walked away carrying a load of some kind. My guess is a sack of gold nuggets and the rifle."

"That's not good news," Randy replied.

"They also found a spot where a boat came ashore two miles down from the crash site. That was his back up plan, I'm sure," Jack said.

"Guys like him are like bad pennies, they just keep coming back to you," Randy observed.

"No doubt I'll run into him again, somewhere on the face of the planet. But I'll be ready next time," Jack answered confidently.

Kitty Koo let out a big meow and jumped on top of the dining table.

"I guess I better go find you a fish," Gwennie smiled.

"I bet I've got one in the kitchen," Adi offered. She scooped up Kitty Koo and walked away.

"Hey, Dad, where to next?" R.O. asked as he walked up to Jack. The crowd got quiet when they heard the question and everyone looked at Jack.

"Well, I've got a few options. There's a couple of threatened species that I need to study in Australia, and a friend

has invited us to hike the Southern Alps in New Zealand. Then we've got some issues in Mexico and Guatemala that need to be resolved. I don't know. I'll tell you at breakfast in the morning."

"Oh, Dad! R.O. sighed and took a bite of the pineapple Danish in his hand.

"Just as long as it's not wet!" Heather exclaimed and smiled at her father.

REVIEWS FOR THE MACGREGOR
FAMILY ADVENTURE SERIES

Cayman Gold: Lost Treasure of Devils Grotto
Book One

VOYA • *Journal for Librarians* • *August 2000*

"Science fact and fiction based on folklore intertwine in this fast-paced story of pirate gold and adventure. In an increasingly rare story line, the family is intact, with parents who are intelligent and involved in the lives of their children. . . . surely will appeal to older teens—mostly boys—looking for a blend of adventure and a bit of romance."

—Pam Carlson

KLIATT • *Journal for Librarians* • *May 2000*

"In this quick-moving adventure story, teenagers who are expert scuba divers bump up against modern-day pirates. . . . The author, an environmental biologist and college professor, shows his love and fierce protectiveness of natural resources and endangered species. This story is fun to read while making teens aware of environmental issues."

—Sherri Forgash Ginsberg,
Duke School for Children, Chapel Hill, NC

Elephant Tears: Mask of the Elephant
Book Two

VOYA • *Journal for Librarians* • *December 2000*

". . . portrays the teens' relationships with each other and with their parents as wholesome but realistic . . . respectfully depicts the native Africans and their tradition without glossing over their problems . . . descriptive narration is admirable—family-friendly realistic wildlife adventure."

—Leah Sparks

KLIATT • *Journal for Librarians* • *September 2000*

". . . the author weaves an exciting adventure while stressing the importance of protecting the earth's dwindling resources and endangered animals. It is a powerful, enlightening novel that remains exciting without being didactic."

—Sherri Forgash Ginsberg

Falcon of Abydos: Oracle of the Nile
Book Three

"Written for all ages, *Falcon of Abydos* is a thrilling adventure story in which the MacGregor family becomes entangled in an ancient Egyptian mystery stretching from the heat of the Sahara to beneath the surface of the Red Sea. . . . An engaging, action-packed, and memorable techno/thriller for young readers."

—*Midwest Book Review, "Children's Bookwatch"*

KLIATT • *Journal for Librarians* • *March 2002*
"This is the third adventure for the traveling MacGregor family. We find them in Cairo, unearthing secrets that could change the face of the Middle East forever. The series consists of . . . action-packed stories . . . [that] make important political and environmental statements as well as providing pure entertainment. This story is loaded with historical facts, laced with romance and humor; a definite purchase for your library."

—*KLIATT*

Czar of Alaska: The Cross of Charlemange
Book Four

"The novel features a strong family unit with realistic sibling rivalry and respect for parents."

—*School Library Journal*

Sign of the Dragon
Book Five

VOYA • *Journal for Librarians* • *October 2007*
"Well done—nonstop and easily envisioned."

—Pam Carlson

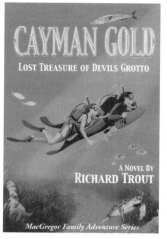

This first novel in the techno-thriller *MacGregor Family Adventure Series* involves sinister pirate forces, strange sea creatures, and hospitable natives, as well as issues of endangered species and environmental management. Suddenly faced with the task of saving a lost Spanish treasure embedded in protected coral reef, the MacGregor teens rely on their courage and scuba-diving skills to explore and investigate the waters and beaches of the Cayman Islands.

In this second novel in the *MacGregor Family Adventure Series,* zoologist Dr. Jack MacGregor again strives to protect the earth's dwindling resources and endangered animals, pursuing an international cartel that is exploiting elephants in East Africa. The family's three teenagers, Chris, Heather, and Ryan, become part of the action and team up with native Africans and a seasoned American aviator to save the animals and bring the exploiters to justice.

In the third and possibly the most chilling challenge for the inimitable MacGregor family, the clan lands amidst the shifting sands of the Sahara Desert to uncover a secret that could forever change the history of Egypt. Just when Egyptologists believe that the last of the great discoveries have been made, the MacGregor family's appearance at the International Environmental Conference in Cairo inspires them to pursue the truth about the Nile River.

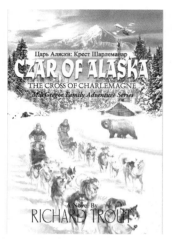

In book four of the *MacGregor Family Adventure Series,* zoologist Jack MacGregor, his paleontologist wife, Mavis, and children, Chris, Heather, and Ryan, are caught in a web of characters pursuing both noble and notorious goals in Alaska. Three Russian Orthodox priests seek the religious artifact the Cross of Charlemagne, while their rivals, a rogue Vatican priest and a renowned Polish archaeologist, threaten to retrieve the treasure first.

In this fifth book in the *MacGregor Family Adventure Series,* Dr. Mavis MacGregor researches the feathered dinosaur while Dr. Jack MacGregor participates in an environmental conference concerning the world's largest dam project, the Three Gorges Dam. Their children, Chris, Heather, and R.O., and Chris's girlfriend, Natalie, explore the Wolong Panda Reserve, where they discover a link between animal exports, the illegal dinosaur bone trade, and corrupt Chinese officials.